Elizabethtown, New Mexico. ca. 1870

Murder in E-Town

A Novel
By Ron Washburn

Although this work is based on actual events, certain liberties have been taken to novelize the story. When possible, the names of individuals who were involved in the events portrayed have been used. Others are fictional, as are some events.

This is copyrighted material and no part of this work may be reprinted or distributed, with the exception of excerpts already released for promotion, without the expressed written consent of the author.

Copyright © 2018 Ronald Jay Washburn
First Edition
The Knights of Altoris Publications
Murder in E-Town by: Ron Washburn
All rights reserved.

ISBN-13: 978-1720848578
ISBN-10: 1720848572

Amazon.com/author/ronwashburn

Get all of Ron Washburn's westerns:
1. The Man From Atlanta
2. Murder in E-Town: A Novel
3. Jornada del Muerto: Cowboys and Monsters
4. Austin's Justice
5. Blue Eyes in the Snow
6. A Reckoning in Goldenburg
7. Journey of Blood: The Lady Gunslinger

All titles available through
Amazon:amazon.com/author/ronwashburn

Dedicated to C. E. Washburn
My father.

Based on a true story.

Prologue

September, 1870.
Palo Fletchado Pass, New Mexico Territory

Tom Pritchett tapped his heels on his pinto horse Águila's side. "Come on, boy. Nice and easy. Don't make no fuss. There ain't no Injuns around." He looked up at the overcast sky and the light snow falling. Palo Fletchado Pass set just about half way between Eagle Nest and Taos on the path that led up from the Moreno Valley and into the Sangre de Christo Mountains in northern New Mexico. The tall pines stretched toward the sky and were already starting to accumulate snow on their branches. The frigid air made Tom shiver in the late afternoon, or maybe it was something else. "We're just there to get a look, maybe a short meal. See if they're alright."

Águila was a surefooted gelding, a mountain horse raised by a mountain man. Tom had just bought him a few months before in the spring from his friend Mike. He was named Águila because of the pattern on his coat that looked like a bird in flight. Tom was pleased at the horse's intelligence and spirit.

As they made their way to their destination, Tom felt a knot growing in his gut. Did he really want to do this? He was on his way to El Paso to spend the winter with his pregnant wife Lorraine and their little daughter Karen. Dealing with what could be a life threatening situation was not on his list of things to do. But, the old man Jose Cortez had begged him. Just a look, see how the young woman and the little boy were doing, that was all. To make sure they were alright. Then he would leave, report what he saw to Jose, and continue his trek south. But it wasn't the woman and little boy's welfare that spooked him. It was what Jose had told him about the woman's husband.

He spotted the unassuming but obvious cabin set up with a water trough, a well-built corral, and a sturdy hitching post out front. A sign clearly read 'Traveler's Rest'. He sighed as the knot in his stomach grew tighter.

"This is it, boy. You just stay right here. I'll be back shortly." He patted Águila's neck and dismounted, looping the reins on the hitching post.

Águila whinnied low, a sort of concerned whinny.

Tom stroked the horse's nose. "I won't be long, boy. I promise."

He heard the front door open, and the form of a large black-bearded man wearing a black suit stepped out.

Tom turned and walked toward him. "Good afternoon, sir. I don't suppose I could get something to eat here? I've got a long journey ahead of me."

"Sure, sure. My wife is just now settin' the table."

Tom stepped onto the front porch, smelling not just the stew inside, but the scent of something rotted. He gulped back his fear and put out his hand. "Tom Pritchett."

The man took his hand and shook it, a powerful grip making it known he was a strong man. "Pleasure to make your acquaintance, Mister Pritchett. Name's Charles Kennedy. Come on in."

Chapter 1

September, 1870.
Elizabethtown, New Mexico Territory

Vigilantes some called us. Or worse. We did what had to be done to insure justice. I'll stand behind that there statement 'till the good Lord calls me and folks start throwin' dirt in my cold, dead face.

It ain't important who I am. If you need a name, then call me Mike Austin. I was just another no-account scoundrel outta the South tryin' to make his way the best way a veteran could. But, like I said before. Ain't none of that important.

What is important is what happened that day when *she* walked in. Right there in John Pearson's saloon in Elizabethtown, or what we called 'E-Town'. Me and Davy Crockett, Clay Allison and the rest of us were there shootin' the shit and drinkin' whiskey. Now, just to clear somethin' up, Davy wasn't the famous frontiersman you might be thinkin' of. He was actually his nephew.

She was a young Spanish woman, bloodied, half frozen to death and scared shitless. The story she told us about the bloody, unholy activities her husband had committed would change our lives forever. But this story ain't about her so much, but about her husband, Charles Kennedy, and how he got what was comin' to him.

Oh, sure. Me and Clay and the rest had earned a reputation for bein' gunslingers and such. But let me set the record straight before we go on. There weren't nobody we shot dead who didn't deserve it.

Anyhow, so there we were, no shit. Just relaxin' in the saloon when this woman stumbled in. She cried and asked for help, that her son had been killed by her husband, and the rest I'm about to tell you. Of course we all got up and helped her, that poor frightened woman. Winter had already arrived, as it usually did in late September in the Moreno Valley. It was freezin' outside and the ground was covered in a couple of inches of snow. She was wearin' a coat that didn't near fit her, and the blood on her was already dried and frozen. Cuts and bruises were all over her arms and face, and it was obvious she'd been through hell. She shivered from the cold and from the trauma she'd suffered.

Whatever saloon shenanigans we were up to at the time stopped dead. We all directed our full attention to her. We sat her down next to the blazin' potbellied stove and gave her some hot coffee to help warm her up. That was when, through tears and shivers, she began her story.

Charles Kennedy was what you might call most of us these days, a mountain man. Pretty much any man who was stout enough to brave the mountains to carve out some kinda livin' was called that, so that in itself weren't so special. It was what he done that stood him apart from good God fearin' folks.

He and his family lived out there in Palo Fletchado Pass, or what we called Taos Pass between Eagle Nest and Taos. He and his wife ran this sort of traveler's rest out of their cabin. Well, turned out, this here traveler's rest would become the *final* restin' place for many an unfortunate traveler.

Kennedy was a big man with a mighty beard. I knew him from a time I had rode through just a few months prior, but I never stopped at his place for long. I don't like imposin' on people, and frankly, I prefer to catch my own food and sleep under the stars, even on the coldest nights. The cold never bothered me. Anyway, I'd seen him out front as I rode by, and yes, I let my horse Stoney, a tough appaloosa, drink some water before continuin' on. Kennedy seemed nice enough. He and I talked some about various subjects, and then he tried to get me to stay a spell. But I wasn't of a mind to. So, I continued on. Probably a good thing I did. It's entirely possible I'da never left.

Missus Kennedy told us how, on that very day, her husband had not only killed another traveler as he ate dinner at their table, but then proceeded to kill her son. It was a horrific scene she described.

See, this here traveler had come in weary from the long trail. Of course Kennedy invited him in, and the Missus set him up with some food. As they all sat around bein' cordial and such, the man asked if they'd seen any Injuns. I hate that term, to be honest with you, but I'm just tellin' you how it went.

Well, then their son said, "Can't you smell the one Papa put under the floor?"

At this Kennedy flew into a hell of a rage. He drew his gun and shot this poor unsuspectin' feller right there on the spot. This not calmin' his rage, he began to take it out on their son, disciplinin' the boy by bashin' his head on the fireplace 'til he was dead.

Now, Missus Kennedy was already terrified of her husband, but she did still try to stop his rage. He beat her severely and made her help drag the bodies of her son and the traveler into the basement. Upstairs, she retreated to a corner in terrified tears as her husband then proceeded to drinkin'. Once he passed out drunk, she made her escape. She ran and ran, 'til she finally stumbled into Pearson's saloon, shiverin' off the cold next to the warm potbellied stove, to tell us this here macabre tale. But that wasn't the end of it. It was only the beginnin'.

We listened as she told us how he'd been inticin' travelers in for years, feedin' them and offerin' them respite. Only thing was, every so often, once he ascertained a traveler had a decent amount of equipment or money, he'd kill 'em and burn their bodies, toss them in a nearby creek, or just bury them around the property or under the house itself. I found this story to be a bit unbelievable, as the stench alone should have alarmed anyone in the vicinity. If you've never experienced the putrid scent of a decayin' human body, well I can tell you. It's a scent that you'd never forget. This is why they need to be buried deep, you see.

I knew that pass well. Many folks stopped by Kennedy's place on a regular basis, payin' two bits for some food and a little bit of watered down whiskey. Everyone knew about him and his Spanish wife and her good cookin'. Surely someone would have noticed somethin' out of kilter. There were rumors that he had a short temper, and even threatened a feller named Coleman with a pistol once. But threatenin' and killin' are two different things.

But, accordin' to her story, he'd been doin' this for years. Nobody ever done nothin' about it, and nobody'd come lookin' for missin' loved ones. I reckoned it made some kinda sense, considerin' most of the folks who traveled on the trail were drifters. Nobody would miss 'em. There was that one judge who went missin' a short time before, but folks just figured he'd gone south to find his fortune elsewhere.

She said there were upwards of fourteen unfortunate souls who'd succumbed to mortality at her husband's hands. Fourteen. Outside of war time, that kinda number of kills is unheard of.

We'd all heard of Charles Kennedy, though. He'd been in some trouble in the area before, not payin' his bills or threatenin' folks at gunpoint, like I said before. Nothin' too spectacular. Certainly nothin' more terrible than our own reputations, if I'm perfectly honest. But if what she said was true, that he'd murdered his own son and so many others just for greed, not to mention beatin' the hell out of his wife, then this man was destined to hang. One thing for sure, I'd be happy to pull that lever or even just put a nice lead ball right between his eyes. If anyone deserved to be shot, he did.

Chapter 2

The saloon was mostly quiet as Missus Kennedy told us her tale. Carmen, one of the nice young ladies who frequented the saloon, produced some bandages and cleaned her up good.

Carmen was a handsome woman in her thirties, long brown hair, black eyes, fair skin, and a nice conformation if you catch my drift. She took Missus Kennedy out of the saloon after cleanin' her up, to her own place and gave her good care. The rest of us sat around the table discussin' the situation.

"String 'im up," I said. "I say we go drag that no good piece of shit out and just stretch his neck right there. Get it done and over with." I drew my gun and checked it, makin' sure it was ready for action. "Or just put a goddamn bullet in his head." I reached up and grabbed the whiskey bottle, takin' a good swig. "Kill him now and let God be the final judge."

"I'm inclined to agree," Davy said. "Come on, let's go get him. Kennedy's cabin is up in Taos Pass. We can get there and have him all strung up and pretty before it gets dark."

Davy was a short, lanky feller. He wore his yellow hair way longer than was respectable, and his scraggly beard made him look like he never liked to take a bath. Or was that his smell? Or was it mine?

I'll admit, I was no better. A week-old beard and longish brown hair, more bones showin' through my skin than should have been. But I could hold my own. I was stronger and taller than most men.

Clay Allison was an intimidatin' man. Not so much a big man, but a man who seemed to command respect just by his personality. And his reputation. He'd done not only some serious work for the Confederacy, but had put down a few no-account scoundrels along the way who didn't see justice the way he did. But make no mistake. Clay never killed no one who didn't need killin'. He and I were synchronized in that philosophy. He wore his brown hair short, had a full beard he liked to keep trimmed, and wore his guns loose and ready. Although he did have a club foot, and a terrible limp which would incite his rage if a feller mentioned it, it never slowed him down.

"We can't go off all halfcocked, fellers," Clay said. "That ain't how we do things."

"No?" I said. "Since when? What about that scoundrel last week that we…" I looked around at the others in the group, and shut my trap.

"Mike. You, me, and Davy will go up there and assess the situation. The rest of you get back to the ranch," Clay said. "We'll handle things here. Tell my brother what's transpiring."

They started protestin'.

"Listen, damn it, if things go sideways, I don't want you fellers involved. Get on back and take care of things. Winter's coming and there are chores to be taken care of. Once we're done here we'll join you. Now do what you're told and skedaddle."

They reluctantly got their things together and left.

"She said he went on a bender," Clay said. "He'll be on the down side of a hangover by now, if not already dead by whiskey. So as soon as the boys clear town, we'll go get Kennedy."

"And string up that son of a—" I said.

"No, Mike. Damn it. That's always your first reaction, ain't it?"

I took a shot of whiskey and scowled. "*My* first reaction? You gettin' all soft now, Clay?"

"Just listen," Clay said. "We'll bring his sorry ass to the jail, all legal and shit. We'll need to look around, too. Find the son and that new feller he killed. Make sure we have evidence. He'll face justice the right way. We need to find that damned deputy too, so he can give this

19

operation his approval. We don't want any of it to be thought illegal."

"I didn't see his horse at his house when I came in. He's probably at Mutz' finishing up that table he made for them," Davy said. "Want me to go get him?"

"Maybe," Clay said. "But you don't know for sure that he's there."

"I can go look."

Clay chuckled. "Then what? Get him to chase you? You know he don't like you after that incident at Lambert's."

Davy snickered.

I shook my head. "It don't feel right is all I'm sayin'. If we do this all legal, with the deputy in tow, Kennedy'll go to trial. And then what? They'll bring in all them high dollar lawyers and shit, and get him off on some kinda technicality."

Clay shook his head. "If so, then he'll meet an untimely accident on his way home."

I smiled. "Damn right."

"But first we give the law a chance."

"I think Mike's right," Davy said as he shook his head. "Don't give him a chance to be cleared. If we get caught helpin' this bastard meet with an unfortunate accident after the law says he's innocent, then *we'll* face the gallows. But if we administer some vigilante justice, the most we'll get is a night's stay in the county's finest accommodations. Especially if we're good and drunk when we do it." He took the bottle and swallowed down a good gulp. "Then we can blame it on the whiskey."

"That's all I was tryin' to say," I said. I looked at Clay. "You know, there was a time I'd be the one tryin' to calm you down, Clay. And it ain't like Kennedy don't deserve it."

"Damn right," Davy said.

"Boys, all we have now is a woman with a story. We don't know if any of it's true, and we don't wanna go having an unjust lynching, at the very least. Hell, she must 'ave walked all night to get here. That's halfway across the mountain. We need to be sure is all I'm saying. Go check things out. See if what she was saying has any truth to it. If so, we can bring in the drunk bastard and be good, upstanding citizens helping the law. We have a good thing going here. A fine ranch, some good friends. Let's try not to get run out of this brand new county on a rail. We already got enough trouble brewing with the Maxwell Grant. We don't need this shit too."

I chuckled. "On a rail. Like that would happen."

"And anyway, the pass is a good fifteen miles as the crow flies," Clay said, "and that ain't exactly an easy ride coming up outta the valley. Just getting there before sundown would be a neat trick, Davy."

"So, what are you sayin'?" I asked. "That we shouldn't go now? You just said a minute ago that we'd go as soon as the boys left town."

Clay took off his hat and scratched his head, like he always did when he was about to lose his temper. "Damn it, Mike! Why you gotta paint me in a corner like this?!" He threw a shot glass at the wall. It shattered.

"I ain't doin' no such thing, Clay. Let's just head out. We'll make good enough time to get there, and then we can discuss what to do along the way," I said.

"Hang 'im," Davy said.

I pointed at Davy and raised my eyebrows.

Clay chuckled and put his hat back on. "Come on. Let's go."

Now, the road up through the mountains was not one where a person'd haul ass, so to speak. Down through the valley the road was covered in snow, and then goin' up towards the pass it got pretty bad in places. You'd have to watch where you were goin'. Plenty of folks had gone through over the years, so it was a well-worn road, but that didn't mean fellers didn't meet their end by a not-so sure-footed horse or mule they didn't drive properly. It took us the rest of the day to get up around where Kennedy had his traveler's rest.

It was an unassumin' little log cabin, two-roomed, like most any you'd see in these parts, but there was a good sized water trough in front and a hand-written sign with the words, 'Traveler's Rest' hangin' from his front porch. Smoke rose from the chimney, which in itself wasn't all that unusual, especially as late September in these mountains was already damn cold. The strange part was that it smelled more like burnin' meat than so much juniper.

"That ain't a good sign," Clay said.

"You don't suppose he's trying to burn up his new victims, do you?" Davy asked.

"I reckon we'll find out," I said.

"Think he'll put up a fight?" Davy asked.

"I sure hope so," I said.

Clay shook his head. "Let's just approach this nice and civilized this time, okay? Not like that last incident. Remember what happened."

"Who the hell are you, and what have you done with my friend Clay?" Davy asked in a chuckle.

So, we rode up to the hitchin' post at the water trough and dismounted.

"Just let me do the talking," Clay said.

"Since you're the big time rancher and all? Think you got some kinda clout with a no-good murderer?" I asked.

"Sometimes you're just a foul person, Mike," Clay said.

Davy nudged me. "You do have a temper, Mike. That's a fact."

I drew my gun and checked the caps, good to go. "What is it you're tryin' to say?"

"I'm just saying, sometimes you tend to ask questions last."

Clay shushed us as we climbed the steps. "Would you two knock it off? You do remember why we're here, right?"

I nodded and put my attention on the door.

Davy drew his gun.

"Just keep them hoglegs in their holsters for now. Jesus," Clay said. "Damned ruffians."

I smelled the distinct scent of rottin' flesh. "I smell death."

"This ain't gonna end well," Davy said, shakin' his head.

Clay knocked on the door. "Mister Kennedy, are you in there? It's Clay Allison come over from E-Town."

The gun shots and the shatterin' wood around our heads was a damn good indication that he not only knew who we were, but why we were there. We ducked and ran down the steps, jumpin' behind a wood pile out front. Our horses spooked and trotted off a few steps.

"Ask questions last, huh?" I said to Davy.

"Get yourrr asshess out ah off en my property!" Kennedy screamed in drunken slurs at us, and then shot a few more rounds through the door.

"Damn flimsy construction for a door," Davy said. "Bullets are going right through it. What do you think that is, thirty six caliber? It shouldn't be able to go through so easily."

"It's enough to put us in the ground!" Clay yelled as random gun fire blasted our general direction.

"So, what? Wait 'till he runs out of ammo like we did with Olson?" I asked. "We waited all night for that bastard. You can't tell me Kennedy ain't armed and ready for an assault."

Davy shook his head. "Too bad we didn't bring some of your dynamite, Mike. We could just toss one stick in there and be done with it."

"I ain't got no more of it," I said. "Sold it to them new prospectors in June."

He chuckled. "That just figures."

"Well, I didn't have any need for it. I'd rather have a full wallet and some good whiskey than some old dynamite that could kill me if I dropped it."

"So, your claim never did too well, huh?" Davy asked. "Is that why you hired on with Clay?"

"That, and herdin' cattle is a hell of a lot easier than diggin' and pannin' all damn day for two bits of gold dust. I'd just had this feelin' when I started, you know. Like there was a good vein of it right under my feet—"

More bullets whizzed by.

"I swear you two talk too much. There's a murdering bastard shooting at us, or did you forget?" Clay asked.

"Nah, we're just waitin' him out," I said. "Just like Olson." I grinned.

Clay took off his hat and scratched his head as another bullet whizzed by. "We ain't waiting," he snarled.

"Now, Clay, maybe you oughta calm down first," Davy said. "Don't go off all halfcocked." He smiled and winked at me.

I shook my head. "Ah, hell. Here we go."

Clay ignored him. He stood straight up and fanned his revolver hammer back, firin' all six shots into the door. "If you're still alive in there, I'd advise you to come on out before we drag your sorry ass out! Do it now, god damn it!" Bullets whizzed by, but he was unaffected. He crouched back down. "God damn son of a bitch."

I grinned at Davy. "There's Clay. Glad he could make it to the party."

Davy chuckled.

"You boys go around back. I'll draw his fire," Clay said.

I shook my head. "Typical. Alright. I'll take right."

Davy nodded and we took off runnin' like our asses were on fire. Gun shots sounded from the house, shatterin' more of the door. No slug came anywhere near us, but we still ducked as we ran.

Clay drew his other gun and commenced to firin' right into the door until his guns were out of ammo. "I said come on out, or by God we'll come in there and drag you out by your neck!"

It was quiet for a few moments as I stooped low, below the shudders, and circled around. Clay would be takin' this time to reload, as I suspected Kennedy would be doin'. But as I peeked around the back, I heard Davy call out and shoot.

"He's getting away!" Davy yelled.

Sure enough, that bastard Kennedy was on a familiar horse, well, halfway on, and the horse was runnin' at full speed into the forest, kickin' up muddy snow as he ran. I raised my gun, but there was no damn way I'd hit him without hittin' that horse. "Son of a bitch!" I said. "That's Tom Pritchett's horse!" It was a tall gelding, standin' probably sixteen hands, a pinto with a unique pattern on his rump that looked like a bird in flight. "That's ole' Águila!"

Davy kept shootin'.

"Davy, stop! You'll hit the horse!" I yelled.

He stopped, but only 'cause he was out of ammo.

Clay came runnin' around. "You let him get away!"

I chuckled. "Nah. That's Águila. He used to be my horse. He'll go about a quarter mile and then turn around. He won't go far without Tom." I turned toward Stoney and whistled so loud it caused Davy and Clay to cringe.

"Damn it!" Clay socked me in the arm. "Warn a person next time!"

"If Tom didn't sell that horse, it probably means he's in the house," I said. "And Kennedy killed him."

"Tom from El Paso?" Davy asked. "The only feller I'd ever seen who could drink you under the table besides Clay? That Tom?"

I nodded. After a few moments, Stoney trotted up to me. "I'll go get Kennedy," I said. I hopped on Stoney and yelled, "Heeeeyyyaaaah!"

"How the hell does he do that?" Davy asked.

"He's got a way with horses. Always has," Clay said as he shook his head.

Stoney could run like few horses could. I hunkered down over his neck, and he burst into a full run. Now, runnin' a horse through forest isn't necessarily a good idea, especially in wintery conditions. Low hangin' branches, sharp sticks that could ruin a horse's hoof, unseen holes, and other hazards that could ruin your day permanently were abundant. But Stoney wasn't just any horse. He was a veteran like me. We'd done our share of this sort of thing- runnin' down folks though the forest who didn't want to get caught.

Charles Kennedy was every bit a mountain man as I was, even in the worn out black suit he was wearin' like some kinda preacher. But he knew how to run from someone like me. I could see him up ahead, directin' Águila to go around obstacles that I didn't realize were there. He knew this area better than me. At the same time he glanced back at me and tried to steady his gun to shoot. But what he didn't know was, that horse he was on didn't like him. Just as Kennedy was about to get a good bead on me, Águila decided the joyride was over. He spun around in mid-stride like the cattle-cuttin' horse I trained him to be. Kennedy went off and onto the ground in a thud. Águila came runnin' up to us.

"Whoa, boy," I said to Stoney. He slowed down to a walk and then a full stop, barely winded as Águila, his old friend, came trottin' up with his saddle halfway off. They whinnied to each other in greetin'. I dismounted and approached Águila. "Easy, boy. Remember me?"

His ears were out toward me as he sniffed and snorted. I petted his neck. The two horses also sniffed and snorted each other. I petted Águila some more, and then straightened the saddle. "You two go on back. I have a scoundrel to catch." I patted Águila on the rump, and he trotted off back toward the cabin with Stoney right after him.

I began walkin' toward Kennedy. "Kennedy! Are you hurt? Did that little olc' horse throw you?"

I heard a gunshot, and a bullet whizzed by my head. I ducked behind a tree. I could just see him about twenty yards away, staggerin' to stand behind a tree too.

"Leave meeees ashlone gods sdamned it!" he said, still obviously drunk, as he fired again.

I ducked. "Now Charley, you best just put that gun down before you hurt yourself. Sounds like you've had a bit too much whiskey. Let me get you some hot black coffee and some food, how 'bout it?"

"Leave mees alone!" he yelled.

A couple more bullets whizzed by.

"Come on, now. All I want is to fix you up and get you to safety. You remember me, it's Mike Austin. We met a while back."

"Youuu gosddamned it! You done it!" he yelled.

"Done what?"

"You done it, and Imma gonna tell 'em all!"

"Charley, I don't know what you mean, but we can sit on down and talk about it. Let's just head on back to your place. Whaddya say?"

"You're a devil in disguise, Mike Austin! You're evil! Like all of them! Damned evil cowards from Hell!" At least he said them words clearly.

Another bullet whizzed by my head. He had one left. I holstered my gun.

"Damn it, Charley! Stop this shit! Your wife already done told us what you did! Now give up like a man!"

Another bullet, and then a click.

I rushed at him as he tried like hell to get his empty gun to fire, but the damn thing was insistent that it didn't want to without more ammo. Stubborn little bastards, them guns are.

He dropped the gun and stood as steady as he could, his fists up ready to beat the holy hell outta me. I ducked slightly and hit him in his midsection with my shoulder, causin' us both to fall. He hit hard, and I thought I heard somethin' snap. He managed to get a neck lock around me, and I was pinned for a moment as he punched me hard in the face. We rolled around in the snow as I pushed my arms around his and forced him to let go. I rolled off him, but then was met with a large stick in the head. He swung it at me as best he could, and I backed away. I felt a lump beginnin' to grow, and was gettin' a bit perturbed by this. I jumped back up just as he hit me again with the stick. This time, though, I managed to grab it. We struggled for a time, playin' a sort of angry tug-o-war 'til he dropped it and swung around with a fist, it barely missin' my nose. Then I hit him as hard as I could in the stomach, but he was just too damn big! He smiled and punched back, knockin' the air outta me. I stumbled back.

"Bastard!" He yelled. "Comin' onto my property and attackinggggsss me! What right do you have?!"

"We know what you did, Charley. Now come along peacefully and face it like a man."

31

"Like a man, huh?" He staggered and looked at me with one eye, as if he only wanted to see one of me. "What would you know about that, you demon?!"

"If anyone's a demon it's you!"

"It was her, that damned whore who done sent you out here, ain't it?"

"It weren't no whore, Charley. It was your lovely wife who you beat the hell out of. And she had every right, you piece of shit!" I lunged at him, but he evaded me.

"How dare you judge me!" He lunged at me, but I'd had enough. I kicked him 'tween the legs and he went down. I drew on him. "Now, just stop all this shit, Charley. Don't you move. I got you dead to rights, and you damn well know it."

He rolled around on the forest floor like a prize hog enjoyin' his muddy puddle for a moment.

"I said don't move!" I fired a round into the ground next to him.

He stopped.

"That's better. Now, grab hold of that tree branch and stand up, nice and slow. As much as I wanna plug you right now for what you done, I won't on accounta Clay wants this done all legal-like."

"I'll kill you devil!" he said as he managed, after a few agonizin' minutes, to get to his feet. He lunged at me and nearly lost his footing. "Assshole."

"Shut up and start walkin'," I said. I backed away and left the trail open toward the way we came, my gun pointed at him.

As we approached the cabin I heard somethin' breakin' inside Kennedy's house, and Davy yellin' at Clay, and then Clay yellin' at Davy. I couldn't make it out. Stoney, Águila, and the other horses quietly grazed on the last bits of grass that poked through the snow a dozen yards away. Kennedy stumbled a few times, but a nudge with a stick in his back kept him on task.

A few folks who were passin' by had gathered 'round to watch the festivities, havin' heard the gunshots.

"I'll kill that piece of shit!" Clay raged as he ran out front.

Davy ran out behind him. "I'm with you! But... we have an audience."

Clay saw us walk up and drew his gun, pointin' it right at Kennedy's head. He pulled back the hammer as he approached. "You low down, no good, piece of shit, son of the devil! If anyone deserves this, you do!"

"Clay!" Davy yelled. "No!"

"It seems we have spectators," I said.

We all glanced around as more and more people peered at us.

"God! Damn! It!" Clay said. He removed his hat and scratched his head. He glared at me.

"You go look! Tell me what you see!" He then turned and socked Kennedy so hard he went down and out like a sack of taters. "And tell me we shouldn't just end it right here, right goddamn now!"

I went inside the house, and the smell overwhelmed me. There in the fireplace was the remains of someone's arm still burnin'. There was fresh blood everywhere. I found pieces of bone and hair, the remains of someone's head, still stuck to the fireplace stone. I followed the trail of blood down into the small basement, which looked like it had originally been set up as some kinda root cellar, and what greeted my eyes made them water.

There was a pile of half-buried bodies, bones, a skull, and partially rotted flesh exposed. The smell was much stronger than up top. I looked up and saw why. The floor had been roofed before it had become the floor for the upstairs. This had sealed away some of the smell, but not all. The body of a small boy, his head all but gone, lay near the staircase, his teeth grinnin' at me and his eyes blank and starin' out into oblivion. On the other side of the basement was a pile of goods. Saddles, guns, and so forth. Most of the guns were in poor repair, like Kennedy had not the time to clean them in-between his busy murderin' business.

But then there was my friend Tom. It was him, alright, with a bullet hole in his head. He had been just an honest prospector with a family back in El Paso. I reached down and grabbed what I knew would be there, a letter in progress in his inner pocket. A letter to his two year old daughter and pregnant wife. I remembered talkin' to him up in the mountains as we panned together in the summer, and he told me that he wrote to his family any time he wasn't workin'. He always had a letter in progress in his inner pocket. After he'd finish one and send it off, he'd start another one. He missed them dearly, but was determined to carve out a life for them. He'd located a good producin' gold claim and was doin' alright. In the winter he'd pack up his gear, sell most of his stuff, cash in his gold, and head home to spend the colder months with his family in the warmer south. When spring would come, he'd head back into the mountains to continue on. I'd sold him Águila in May to replace the old mule he'd been usin'. It had died on his way up to the mountains. I'd trained that horse on Clay's ranch.

'I hate being away from my family,' he'd explain to me with tears in his eyes. 'But at least they'll have a good winter and my little girl will have a full belly. I can't wait to hold them in my arms on them cold nights, the stove raging with a nice fire.' He'd always smile when he said this, his eyes starin' off. Last time I'd talked to him he was more than excited to get back to be home to see his little girl and pregnant wife as the new arrival came. She was due in October.

Tears rolled down my cheeks. The rage left me, replaced by grief. I sat down next to my friend and put his hand on mine for a moment.

"A good man who didn't deserve this, leavin' a family behind to fend for themselves. A boy who was just a boy, for God's sake. Why, God, why? Why would you let this happen? They didn't do nothin' wrong. Nothin' at all."

Tom's cold dead eyes stared as if at me. I knew what needed to happen next. Not a lynchin' like I was all hot for before, but justice. Real justice. And a proper Christian burial for these poor souls. All of them. I took the letter and put it in my pocket. I'd take it myself to his family in El Paso. They deserved to hear the truth in person.

And Charles Kennedy deserved to hang after bein' convicted properly in a court of law. The world needed to know what happened here. The right way.

I walked out, still cryin' like a baby. I leaned on the cabin wall and looked up at Clay. "No. We ain't lynchin' him. We're takin' him back where he'll be tried and hanged properly. Then I'll head to El Paso and…" I choked up, unable to speak.

Clay sighed and nodded. He looked around at the folks still watchin'. "Go on home, folks."

Nobody budged.

I secured the bodies of Tom and Kennedy's son, still not knowin' what his name was, on Águila. My soul was full of grief and anger.

Clay and Davy woke up Kennedy with a bucket of water, got him on his feet, and proceeded to tie him up. He didn't resist. He just stood and watched the audience as they watched him.

"I don't like it," Clay said as he tied the rope around Kennedy's neck, and loopin' it through a knot around his wrists. "He should hang here, now."

"Funny how things turn around," Davy said. "You were the one wanting to do things legal. And now, we're the ones holding you back."

"It is the right thing to do to hang him now," Clay said. "And you damn well know it."

I finished tyin' the ropes around the bodies draped over the horse and said, "The world needs to know what happened here, Clay. Not as a vigilante gang doin' a lynchin'. But as good citizens apprehendin' a dangerous criminal to bring him to justice, handed out by a court of law. We owe it to Tom and his family, and sure as hell owe it to Missus Kennedy, and to that poor boy." I walked over and punched Kennedy, nearly breakin' his nose. The fury boiled inside me as tears still rolled down my face. It was all I could do to contain myself. His already bloody face bled some more. I grabbed him by the throat and stared into his soulless eyes, grittin' my teeth in rage. "But if this piece of shit does anythin' to complicate his transport, I wouldn't be opposed to a little early comeuppance comin' his way. I just want to know somethin', Charley. What the hell is wrong with you?! Why would you do this? Tom was my friend! He had a family, people who loved him, counted on him! And your own son? What was your boy's name? Huh? Tell me his name you piece of shit!"

His cold eyes stared back at me. "You don't know nothing, Mike. Nothing at all. You don't know what those folks were. They deserved what they got, for the glory of Heaven is at hand. Shay Lamb is coming! I am the hand of God!"

I squeezed my grip, and he began to choke. "That little boy didn't deserve to have his brains bashed in! What was his name?! Say it!"

Davy pulled at me, "Mike, come on. He'll get his comeuppance. He will. The right way, like you said."

"Let Mike be," Clay said. "Let him squeeze the life from that son of a whore. Show him the true hand of God, Mike. Go ahead. Do it."

My insides felt like they were comin' apart. Part of me knew takin' him in was the right thing to do. But one side felt that killin' him here was what the good Lord demanded. I released him and pulled away, tears pourin' down my face. I shook with grief and rage. As he gasped for air I said, "It is written, vengeance is mine; I will repay, saith the Lord." I turned away and went to Stoney, makin' sure Águila's lead rope was secured on Stoney's saddle horn. I wiped away the tears of hate from my face.

"Romans twelve, nineteen," Davy said. "God will judge you, Mister Kennedy, after a jury convicts you and an Earthly judge sentences you to hang." He spat at him, landin' a nice big glop on Kennedy's bloody nose. It dripped down, mixin' with the blood. "And then God will get his vengeance upon you himself."

Clay snarled. "He'll have all night to think about it before we get back to E-Town." He took the rope and wrapped it around his saddle horn, and then mounted his horse. "This little stroll will sober him up. Let's go, boys." He made a couple of clicks with his tongue and tapped his heals on his horse's belly. As the horse suddenly moved forward, the rope yanked at Kennedy, pullin' his arms in front of him and tightenin' slightly around his neck, forcin' him to either walk, or fall and be dragged. He stumbled but got his feet under him and followed.

Davy and I mounted our horses.

"Let's pick up the pace and see how he likes bein' dragged," I said.

Clay nodded at me. "Sounds tempting. But I think after fifteen miles of walking, he'll feel some pain. A small slice of the pain he's dealt out."

"It ain't enough," I said. My hand itched to pull my gun and end Kennedy right then. "Nowhere near enough."

"What ain't right is you letting them bodies ride, and making me walk," Kennedy said

"Keep talkin', see how you like havin' your tongue cut out," I said as I caressed the handle of my foot long Arkansas Toothpick.

He shut his trap.

We headed out single file. Davy in front, then Clay with Kennedy pulled behind, and then me ponyin' Águila. It was a good plan. If Kennedy tripped and nobody noticed, ah, shucks. 'Didn't mean to trample you with two horses.'

It weren't nearly five miles later he started cryin' for water, stumblin' like he was about to collapse. I looked at him in front of me and grinned in the half-moonlight, just hopin' he'd trip.

"Please, just some water," he pleaded.

"Tough it out, mountain man," I said. "I've had to march a hundred miles in the hot Georgia sun with not but a hint of water from short rainfall. This is nice and cool, you'll be fine."

"You're going to kill me!" he exclaimed.

"I'd really like to, so don't push me."

He straightened out and walked right for another three miles or so, and then he stumbled and fell on his ass. I chuckled as he scooted along the trail for a few feet, chokin' on the tightenin' rope.

"Damn it, hang on," Clay said. He stopped as we all did. He dismounted and grabbed his canteen. "If we're going to do this, we should at least be Christian about it." He walked up to Kennedy and helped him up. "Drink."

I nodded. "Christian. Sure. We can nail him to a tree. How'd that be for Christian?" I snarled.

Clay looked at me and shook his head. He knew I wasn't kiddin'. He'd seen me do worse. I'd seen him too. And Davy, hell. I'd seen him wipe out an entire saloon who made fun of his name. I sat there and considered these facts as Kennedy stood there before me. What the hell were we holdin' back now for? Why should now be any different? He deserved the absolute worst the three of us could come up with. Yet, somethin' told me we needed to pursue our present course of action.

Kennedy grabbed the canteen as best he could and chugged it down, nearly chokin' on it. Clay loosened up the slip knot around the scoundrel's neck a bit.

"Please, it's another ten miles to E-Town. I can't make it, it's too far," Kennedy pleaded. "Let me ride. At least for a little while. I won't try nothing, I promise as God is my witness."

"My hog barn was about ten miles from my house," I said. "Before the Yankees burned it all down. I walked that distance every day just to

41

feed the hogs. And that was before breakfast. Stop whinin'."

Clay chuckled. "Up-hill both ways, I'd wager."

I tried not to smirk. "In four foot high snow in the winter."

"Of course." He took back the canteen. "You're just dehydrated from all that whiskey. Look at Mike there. He downed a whole bottle before we came out to fetch you, and he never even staggered. No rides. Walk. You deserve it." He mounted up, and we continued on.

Kennedy looked back at me in desperation, as if that would get me to change my mind.

I reached into my vest pocket and produced my whiskey flask. I opened it and took a nice, healthy gulp as the rope yanked him back in line. I grinned. "Ahhh. Good ole Tennessee whiskey. Ain't nothin' better."

"You're a monster, Mike," Kennedy said as he struggled to walk. "God will have his revenge on you for your deception."

I chuckled. "Oh, I'm the monster, huh? I have no idea what the hell you're talkin' about."

"You will. Someday."

I shrugged. "Well, alright then. But you'll get yours first."

"In Hell," Clay said as he reached down and yanked on the rope, causin' Kennedy to nearly fall again.

Clay, me, and Davy laughed.

He complained, but never fell again until we were at the E-Town jail house. There wasn't any light inside.

"It's about midnight," I said. "Deputy Houx could be anywhere. Probably done gone home."

"Probably at Middaugh's saloon," Clay said. "About half lit."

"I'll go get 'im if he is," Davy said. He turned his horse and trotted off that direction.

"Davy, no making him dance with gunshots to the feet. You need to stop doing that to law enforcement types," Clay said. "We need him on our side this time."

"You're no fun at all," Davy said.

"Maybe he's just home with his wife," I said. "Readin' law books or fixin' a desk."

"On a Saturday night? Not likely," Clay said.

Kennedy collapsed. His boots were worn nearly through.

I kicked him on the bottom of his foot. "Get up."

"You'll all get what's comin' to you," Kennedy warned, just before he vomited a most rank puddle.

I turned away. "Jesus, boy."

Clay yanked on the rope. "Come on, get on in there." He pushed open the door to the jail house.

Kennedy stumbled in, managin' to get hold of one of the jail bars inside.

I lit up a lamp.

The jail house was nothin' more than a single room, stone wall buildin'. There were two jail cells on one end, makeshift bars made of scrap iron attached to the roof and floor frames, and no windows except for the one near the front door. A single wood cot sat in each cell bolted to the wood floor, no mattress or anythin' else. The deputy's desk sat at the opposite end of the room. There was a good half inch of dust over everythin'.

Clay shoved Kennedy into a cell and pulled the door closed. The lock was nothin' more than a chain around the door and the frame, with a regular pad style lock. He snapped it shut. "Come here and let me get that rope off of you."

Kennedy staggered up, his hands out. "Could I please have some water now?"

"Maybe," Clay said. He untied him. "If you sit down and keep your mouth shut." He walked out with the rope.

I opened the water jug and dipped out some into the deputy's coffee cup, and then handed it to Kennedy. "Not that you deserve it."

He grabbed it and chugged it down. "Thank you."

I took the cup back and sat it on the desk. "Better get some rest, Charley. If deputy Houx is in the saloon, you won't see nobody but me for a good spell."

"Is there any kind of… mattress, or blankets?" It's cold. At least start a fire."

"Tough it out, mountain man." I sat at the chair, put my feet up on the desk, and tipped my hat forward. "Ahh, this is a comfortable chair." I was snorin' in no time.

I awoke to somebody knockin' my boots off the desk. I immediately stood with my gun in hand, ready for trouble. Sunlight shown through the open door. I saw three silhouettes. If I was fast enough, I could take out all three before they had a chance to draw.

"Easy, there, partner," Clay said. "It's us. Put that hogleg away 'for someone gets killed. Why didn't you start a fire?"

I sighed and holstered my gun. "Damn it, Clay. You know better'n to wake me like that."

Davy chuckled. "I said so."

Deputy Houx walked up to the jail cell. He was a tall feller, and stout. He wore the typical clothes, with a grey hat, and a black vest adorned with a deputy star on it. "What did you do to him?" He asked as he looked in on Kennedy.

Kennedy sat on the cot, the blood on his face all dried up, and multiple bruises. He shivered. "They tried to kill me, Marshal."

"I'm a deputy. You know who I am, Mister Kennedy. And I suspect if they'd wanted you dead, you would be." He turned to us. "It ain't going to help that you beat the hell out of him."

"I never touched him," Davy said.

"Me neither," I said.

"Nor I," Clay said.

Houx scowled. "Why don't I believe you?"

"He tripped and fell is all," Clay said.

"Yeah?"

"Yeah."

"Then that would make sense, seeing as you dragged him." Houx pointed. "I see them marks on his hands and neck, Clay. This is your style."

Clay shrugged. "We apprehended a dangerous criminal and brought him in, all legal and shit."

"All legal and shit, huh?"

"Yes, sir. Deputy, sir."

Houx shook his head. "After I get some cure for this hangover I'll send for the Sheriff. See what he wants to do next. I do believe you boys did the right thing bringing him in, but you could have been a bit more, I don't know. Humane about the whole thing. And you shoulda asked me first."

I scowled. "Humane? Go see his place. See them bodies I brought. Then talk to me about what humane means."

"I took care of that stuff for you, Mike," Clay said, but I didn't hear him through my rage.

"Could I please get some food, and water, and… I could use a trip to the outhouse," Kennedy said.

Houx looked at him. "We'll take care of you, Mister Kennedy." He looked at me. "Seems you're the new sub-deputy, Mike. You take care of him. Get a fire going in that stove and escort him to the outhouse. And no shenanigans!" He looked at Davy and Clay. "You two, come with me."

I sighed. "God damn it."

Houx spun around with his finger pointed at me. "Don't you take the Lord's name in vain in my jail, understand?!"

I backed up. "Yes, sir, Deputy, sir!" I saluted.

He shook his head. "Smart ass. I'll have some breakfast sent over for the both of you."

Chapter 3

Takin' Kennedy to the outhouse was an uneventful occasion. All I did was unlock the cell, pointed my gun at him and said, "Outhouse is out back. It's your choice. Please try to escape." I waved him out, no chains or restraints of any kind. He was compliant. I followed him out, waited for him to complete his business, and then followed him back. No trouble whatsoever, unfortunately. Yes, I started a dam fire to keep Kennedy warm. Hell, it was day time. It wasn't that cold anymore. What did he need it for, anyway? I did what I was told, though.

Carmen showed up soon after with two plates of food and a full pot of coffee.

"Oh, sweet Jesus," I said as I smelled it all. Scrambled eggs, bacon, toast. God's own hands must've cooked them, 'cause they smelled perfectly divine. Or maybe that was Carmen.

"Hello, Mister Austin," she said with a smile. "The deputy said you'd be needing some breakfast." She sat my plate down on the desk and walked over to Kennedy. Her whole demeanor changed immediately. "And here's your food, you sack of shit." She as much as tossed it at him through the food slot at the bottom. A slice of bacon bounced out and onto the floor. "I hope you choke on it."

He knelt down and picked it up. "Do I get a fork for these eggs?"

"You got two hands," she said, and spun around to me. Her dark, hateful expression then lightened up. "So, Mister Austin. How is it? I cooked it myself." She grinned wide, and I saw her single dimple on the right cheek deepen.

Lord have mercy she was a handsome woman, alright. Downright beautiful. I grabbed the fork she had provided me and dug in. Oh, yeah. Damn tasty. I smiled and nodded at her. "They're perfectly divine, my dear. Thank you ever so much."

Her grin somehow widened, and I think she may have blushed. Her cheeks grew slightly red. She gave me a little shy shrug and said, "Maybe when the deputy relieves you, you can come see me. Bring them plates back."

I must have been grinnin' pretty wide too. "Sure thing, Miss Carmen. I'll surely do that."

She giggled a little and exited, glancin' at me one more time before closin' the door behind her.

I felt the desire for sin in my heart, and improper thoughts began to invade my mind. "I'll take your plates back, alright," I whispered to myself.

"She's a beautiful young woman," Kennedy said. "You two would make a fine couple."

There went the mood, right into the damn outhouse. "You just keep your trap shut, Charley." I ate my breakfast, pourin' myself a nice strong cup of coffee.

"Too bad about she being a whore and all," he said just quiet enough that I almost didn't hear him.

Rage suddenly exploded in my mind. I jumped up, gun in hand, and ran to the cell. "I said shut your god damn trap!" I cocked the hammer. "I'll kill you where you sit!" I pointed the gun right at his head.

He chuckled. "You don't fool me, Austin. You may have killed in the war, but you would never kill an unarmed man, prone in a cell like this. You got scruples. I can see it. Just wait until Father Draugar gets a hold of you and your Thohca. You'll see. This weakness of yours will be your undoing. Shay Lamb is coming, and there's nothing you can do to stop it."

"What the hell are you talkin' about? Damn nonsense. I *should* put you out of your misery. But, you're right about somethin'. I do have scruples." I decocked the gun and holstered it. "Unlike you."

He glared at me as he shoved handfuls of food into his filthy mouth. "I'll walk out of this cell a free man, Austin. You can't prove I did anything wrong. I didn't kill them folks. My wife did it. All I did was try to clean up the mess. But then..." His head dropped and he began to cry. "But then she killed our son. I tried to stop her, but, she was crazy!"

I shook my head. "You're the crazy one, Charley. You'll hang, alright. Or I *will* put a bullet in your head. One way or 'nother, you'll be standin' before Saint Peter soon enough." I returned to my breakfast and just stared at it. I'd lost my appetite. I pushed away the plate and glared at Kennedy.

After a few more minutes, Deputy Houx walked in lookin' more like a deputy and less like a whiskey drinkin' degenerate. "Mike, come on outside for a minute."

"I didn't hurt him, Deputy. But I wanted to," I said as I stepped outside.

"You're relieved of jail duty for now," he said. "But we may have a problem."

"Jesus, now what?"

"The only witness we have is his wife. And to be honest, you fellers apprehended him illegally. You invaded his home without legal authority to do so, and hunted him down like a wild animal, practically dragging him to E-Town against his will. That's kidnapping. But, I'll try to make it seem like you acted under my orders."

I rubbed my forehead in frustration. "Deputy, maybe you should go see what we seen. I have two bodies I need to get in the ground, too. What more evidence do you want?"

"See, that's the other thing. You disturbed the crime scene. I did go look last night after I heard what happened, with the boys, while you slept in that chair. I saw what you saw. But…it may not be enough."

"Christ, this is ridiculous. He killed them people, Deputy!"

He shook his head. "Just go on, take care of them bodies. I'll wait here until I hear from Sheriff Calhoun. And…Kennedy's wife wants to talk to you. All of you." He sighed. "Either way, I'll cover you."

"Unbelievable," I said as I walked off.

"Stay out of trouble, Mike!" he yelled after me.

Stay out of trouble. Me. All I wanted to do was make sure justice was served. I mean, sure. I was as rowdy as the next feller. I sure had my time shootin' up towns and such, but I was never in 'trouble' as he said. I mean, hell. Other than Camp Sumter, I hadn't been in any kind of jail for more than a week in my whole life. I supposed the deputy was right, though. Seemed the world was changin'. A lynchin' wasn't what we needed now. What we needed was lawful justice. Especially around these parts. E-Town was growin' fast with all the prospectors, me included. I had a little claim up near Baldy, but it never panned much. I had gotten enough to keep me in whiskey 'till I met Clay and we discovered we'd crossed paths before in the war. Southerners tend to stick together. So, I started helpin' him with his cattle ranch instead of pannin' gold. It was almost a day's ride to his place out between the rivers. But, he paid me better than pannin' ever did.

Today I thought about Charley as I walked toward the livery. Mister Kennedy and what he done. Poor Missus Kennedy. I couldn't imagine what that poor young woman had gone through. She couldn't have been more than eighteen years old, and she had to live with this evil bastard twice her age. To have to deal with his killin' and try to raise a son too must have been horrible, I reckon so. I sure wasn't lookin' forward to talkin' to her.

I reckoned Clay had taken care of the horses and such. I vaguely remembered him sayin' so at the jail. I was too busy nappin' in the jail house while Charley whined and complained about his accommodations. I walked into the livery to see Jeff Ericson, the livery and blacksmith feller, talkin' to Tim Burleson the undertaker.

Jeff was a big man, probably around six feet tall or better, with big muscles and a long red beard. Most of the time he wore only short pants as he hammered out horseshoes and things on his forge, not worried about the stray ember. He had plenty of little scars to show just how little he cared about it. I suppose, as much as the cold didn't bother me, the heat didn't him.

Tim was a short, chubby man who always seemed to be tryin' to adjust his posture like his momma was right behind him with a switch. He wore the typical undertaker's uniform. Long black coat and tall top hat like he was some kinda aristocrat.

I saw Stoney and Águila busy crunchin' on some oats in nearby stalls. They both noticed me and gave a little acknowledgin' whinny. God help me, I love horses. There are two things that get my hackles up about evil men. One, raisin' a hand to a woman or a child. Two, doin' the same to a horse. I'd killed men for it, back when the law wasn't so prevalent.

My mind went back to Texas just four years before when the infamous 'El Loco' Santiago Sanchez was gunned down in the middle of Stanton. Son of a bitch deserved worse, but I suppose the entire Diaz family emptyin' their guns into him was good enough. He'd been killin' little girls all the way from Agua Dulce to El Paso. Damn near got Flora, Miguel Diaz' grown daughter, killed too. Another man named Clay I was friends with had lost a damn good horse that day. May Rex rest in peace.

God help any man who hurts a woman, child, or horse. My anger rose again, rememberin' the current situation. I wanted more than anythin' to put that Charley Kennedy down. But, we had other things to think about.

"Mister Austin?" Tim asked. "You the one that brought them two bodies?"

"Yep."

"Well, I need some kinda identification," he said. "Who's the boy?"

"I don't know his name. The man is Thomas Pritchett, from El Paso."

"Do you know their birthdates?"

"Tom was born in 1838, and I suspect the boy is around three years old, maybe a bit younger. I don't rightly know for sure."

"Does Mister Pritchett have any family that needs to be notified?"

I nodded. "A wife and child. But, I'll do that. I'll be headed south soon enough."

"Mister Austin, it's a foregone conclusion the fine folks of this town won't let them be buried in the consecrated ground of the city cemetery. Well, maybe the boy, but not Mister Pritchett."

"I understand. I'll pay for a couple of plots, one in the open ground nearby, if that's alright."

"Fine by me. Plenty of commoners go there. What about Missus Kennedy? Will she have any say in the boy's burial? I mean, she's his mother."

I sighed in grim anticipation. "I'll talk to her first."

"Good enough. I'll have the invoice sent... where are you staying?"

I chuckled. I hadn't made any arrangements to stay anywhere except on my own bedroll. I hesitated. "I'll just come by your office later."

"That'd be fine." He nodded respectfully, his hands folded together, and walked away.

"He sure does give me the willies," Jeff said. He shook almost like a wet dog gettin' the water off his coat. "Anyhow, Clay brought in your horses and took care of talking to the undertaker, but I reckon you figured that out already. Is that Mister Pritchett's horse?"

"Yep. A fine three year old."

"Never seen a Pinto with that kind of markings. You willing to sell him to me? I'll give you a fair price."

"No, thanks. I'm gonna take him to El Paso, give him to Tom's wife. She can sell him or keep him, whatever she wants. It's only right."

"Well, if you change your mind, let me know." He went back to feedin' the horses and doin' the chores.

"Thanks. I need to find Clay and Davy. I reckon they're already saucin' it up."

"I doubt it. Saloons are closed this morning."

"What? Why?"

"Town ordinance, Mike. You know that. No saloons open on Sunday morning."

"Ah, hell. That's right. I forgot what day it was. Too much damned civilization in this town lately."

"So, what are they going to do about that Mister Kennedy?"

"I'm hopin' for a quick trial and a nice public hangin'. This town needs to see what happens to bastards like him."

"I reckon that's true."

"Problem is, the deputy said we done it all wrong. Went and captured him like an animal and all. And no witnesses except for his wife, and that would never stand up in a court of law, or somethin' like that."

"No witnesses? Are you sure? That was out at Palo Fletchado, wasn't it?"

"Yep. His traveler's rest stop."

Jeff shook his head and stopped in the middle of forkin' a pile of hay. "Now wait a minute. Jose Cortez said something the last time he was in here about seeing Kennedy shoot some feller around about Christmastime. Damn it, what was it he said?" He tapped his forehead.

"Wait, you sayin' we might have an unrelated eye witness?"

"Maybe, but... damn if I can remember. That was some time ago, Mike. I've slept since then." He chuckled.

"How long?"

"Been at least six months. I just remember him saying something about a feller running down from Kennedy's place and Kennedy plugging him right in the head. I wasn't really listening, 'cause you know, I hear stories about scoundrels getting their due from time to time. I don't never think nothing about it. I just wanted to get his leaf spring fixed and get on home. Emily... well, you know."

I nodded. "I remember her."

"I just hope she's happy with that big city business man and all."

I laughed. "No you don't. You're hopin' she's miserable so she'll come back to you. Just admit it."

He grinned. "I reckon that's true. Maybe you oughta ride out to Jose's place, see if you can get him to come forward."

"Yep, I think I might just do that. But for now, I gotta track down Clay and Davy."

"They probably went on home, Mike. That's half a day's ride to Clay's ranch, and I'd bet they're already in Cimarron by now. No reason to stick around here. Especially on a dry Sunday morning."

I nodded. "You're probably right. Just the same, I oughta find Missus Kennedy and talk to her about her son and all." I turned to walk out.

"Let me know if you change your mind about that horse, Mike."

I chuckled as I left. "I will." But I wouldn't change my mind. It was made up. Tom's wife was now the rightful owner. No doubt about that.

The church bells started ringin' as I made my way toward 'Carmen's Massage Parlour.' Was God tryin' to tell me somethin'?

Maybe.

As I crossed paths with folks all dressed up and on their way to church, the thought occurred to me that scoundrels like me might be the ones who God picked to do his dirty work. I stopped and thought about it for a moment. It would be easy. I could go relieve the deputy as he waited for Sheriff Calhoun to return from wherever he'd gone. Then just... No. Kennedy was right about somethin', after all. I had scruples. Well, at least a couple, anyway.

I stepped into Carmen's, and the place was pretty quiet. Carmen sat at her desk as a couple of lady 'masseuses' dressed in questionable attire sat on the couches rubbin' emery boards over their nails. They all looked at me as I entered, with smiles on their faces, until they saw who it was. I reckon they all knew I was Carmen's.

The place itself was set up as a fancy parlour, like all the establishments of ill repute were, to be perfectly honest. Soft couches, lacey and colorful drapes and decorations, the works. And it all smelled strongly of lavender.

"Mike!" Carmen said with just a little bit too much excitement. Her wide smile faded a bit as she got her composure back. "So, you forget something?" She looked at my hands.

"Shit. The dishes. I reckon I did." I removed my hat.

"Good thing I didn't leave you with my fine China, you saddle tramp," she said as she winked.

"I can't deny that. Say, Carmen, I need to talk to Missus Kennedy, see where she wants her boy buried."

Her smile vanished. "Damn shame, Mike. Just a damned shame. We should just string that bastard up right now."

"As much as I'd like to, Deputy Houx wouldn't have it."

"She's in the Lambert Inn," Carmen said. "Henry's being so kind as to put her up. I guess Clay said he'd pay for it."

Several of the ladies made an almost inaudible giggle at Clay's mention.

"He can be a gentleman when he wants to. Especially to the ladies."

"Maria Gregoria."

"Huh?"

"Missus Kennedy. Her name is Maria Gregoria."

I chuckled. "Maria. Yeah, she and most of the Spanish women in this country." I nodded and turned to the door. "Thanks, Carmen."

"Hey, saddle tramp. You still owe me some dishes. Maybe you can help me clean 'em." She giggled, along with all the ladies.

I opened the door. A cold wind was blowin', and the sky looked dark. A winter storm was brewin'. "A storm's a comin'," I said. I turned and smiled at her. "I just might take you up on that." I winked, put on my hat, and walked out.

Lambert's Inn was probably the best place to stay if a person had the money to do so, I mean, other than the Mutz. It was by far one of the best constructed buildin's in E-Town, and had a bunch of rooms. Not sure how many, but a bunch, and they were set up nice and fancy.

The desk clerk pointed me in the right direction, and soon I stood in front of Missus Kennedy's door. I took a deep breath and knocked.

There was no answer.

"Missus Kennedy... er... Maria? It's Mike Austin. We met at Pearson's Saloon, remember?"

She tentatively opened the door. She stood with it partially open, studyin' me with those black eyes. "What is it, Mister Austin?"

"Missus Kennedy, may I come in? It's a bit awkward talkin' out here."

She opened the door and stepped back. She was terrified, I could see it on her face. She had been cleaned up properly by Carmen, and was wearin' a respectable dress. I stepped in and pushed the door open so it was fully ajar, and quickly removed my hat. "Missus Kennedy... may... may I call you Maria?"

She shrugged like this name would do just as well as any other.

"Maria. I have your son's body... actually the undertaker does. Where do you want him buried?" I blurted it out, with no tact and not one bit of class. I cursed myself.

Her lower lip quivered, and her eyes filled with tears. Her whole body began to shake. "Mijo. Mi Samuelito," she said quietly.

"Ma'am... I'm so sorry. I mean... I just... damn my mouth." I shook my head.

She suddenly hugged me tight, to my surprise. She began heavin' in tears, cryin' hard as you would expect a woman who had been treated like she had, who had just lost her son at the hands of that no good Charles Kennedy. I closed my arms around her, comfortin' her as best I could as my own rage burned inside. This wasn't right. Not one damn bit.

"Mi Samuelito!" she cried.

As God was my witness, Charles Kennedy would pay for what he done. One way or another.

Chapter 4

I let the undertaker know that Samuel was to be buried in the cemetery, as I had suggested. Missus Kennedy had said somethin' about puttin' him next to the garden at her home, but she changed her mind pretty quick when I explained what kind of legal battle we were facin'.

The rest of the day was somber, to say the least. Missus Kennedy was sequestered in her room at the Lambert Inn, and I had a mission to find the witness. So I got Stoney, packed him up for an overnight trip just in case, and headed out once again toward Taos. Jose Cortez lived out that way, well sometimes. He was kind of a drifter who spent some of his time in these parts doin' odd jobs and such. But I knew when he was around he'd be stayin' at an abandoned buildin' near Kennedy's place.

As I rode out of town, white flakes of snow started comin' down in the frigid crisp air. Our breath made a white mist when we exhaled. First of October and the winter had already come on pretty strong. That was about normal in these parts. The smells had changed too. It was a combination of scents, Stoney's normal 'horse' scent, my 'ain't bathed in a week' scent, the sweet pines and the distant chimney fires driftin' up, and so on. Typical wintery smells. I took in a deep breath and let my mind drift for a spell. It was times like these I felt the most at home, no matter where I actually was. There was somethin' about the snow fallin' with the mountains in the distance. It reminded me of home. The word 'Velland' came to my mind when these nostalgic feelin's hit me. Not sure what the word meant, but it was probably some place in Norway my grandfather or someone had told me about when I was a boy. Some place that looked like it did here; mountains all around, trees, and cool air with the snow fallin'.

I reached into my inner vest pocket and pulled out my heirloom coin to look at, the only thing I had from my childhood. It was an ancient silver Norse coin, roughly an inch in diameter. On one side it had the image of a Norse ship, and on the other side it showed a demon or somethin'. Maybe a gargoyle. A terrifyin' man with wings. Norse runes went around the edge that I couldn't read. All I ever knew about it was that it came from the old country. That and the strange word was all I had left of the time before the war. I sighed and put it back.

Stoney snorted at the snow.

"Come on, boy. Let's see if we can get there before a blizzard hits us." I made a click with my mouth, and he picked up the pace.

It weren't near an hour later the snow started comin' down in earnest. It wasn't playin' around no more. Although the cold didn't bother me, I knew Stoney didn't like it much. We moved a little faster 'till we came upon Jose's place nestled in the woods back a few dozen yards from the main trail. I pushed Stoney to gingerly walk up to it as I looked around for activity. There weren't no smoke comin' from the chimney, so that was a good indication of his absence. Just the same, I figured I'd take a closer look. Stoney started browsin' the ground for edibles, knockin' away the accumulatin' snow with his nose.

I dismounted and drew my gun, just in case. I didn't hold it up, though. Snow and gunpowder make a dull combination. I kept it hidden in my vest as I started walkin' around. "Jose Cortez, you in there? It's Mike Austin from E-Town."

There was no response, so I pushed the door open. I peered inside, seein' nothin' but a dark room. Nobody home. I walked on in, just in case I seen somethin' that might illuminate his whereabouts. It wasn't nothin' more than a shanty, an old abandoned herder's house he'd been stayin' in. But there were signs he'd been there recently. The little fireplace was still warm, and there were papers and opened food cans scattered here and there. Then I seen a photograph. A photograph was a rare enough object in these parts. It got my interest. So, I picked it up and looked.

It was of Kennedy and his wife posin', she and him dressed up nice. I guessed it was a weddin' photograph. I turned the thing over and saw the words, 'Para mi Papi Jose' written on the back in delicate handwritin'. My mind scoured through the possibilities, and two came to me. One, Jose was Missus Kennedy's father. And two, she knew how to read and write. If he was her father, it would explain why he stuck around 'till now. But, why didn't he try to get her out of that bastard's clutches? I looked around. Maybe he did and was killed for it. Maybe one of them bodies under their house was his. I looked at the still warm fireplace and put the photograph in my pocket as I left.

As I got back on Stoney I looked the direction of Kennedy's place. Had I missed somethin' that maybe I shoulda been lookin' for? I glanced down at the photograph one more time and made a decision. "Come on, boy. Let's go take another look, just for the hell of it."

As I headed back down toward the main trail, I noticed a little dip in the fallen snow, like a hidden trail through the woods. Had Jose been sneakin' over to Kennedy's to check on his daughter and grandson? It would make a lot of sense.

Within a few minutes I arrived at Kennedy's abandoned cabin. I rode around it, lookin' at the construction and the surroundin' area with a little bit more patience than I'd had last time when we apprehended the low-life. There was a corral, a stable of sorts, and of course the cabin itself. But somethin' struck me as odd. I sat there on Stoney as I looked around. Somethin' seemed out of place, somehow. I looked up toward the area where I'd chased down Kennedy, then back at the cabin, then around at the corral and back at the cabin. What the hell was it? I guided Stoney back to the hitchin' post out front and dismounted. I just stood there for a couple of minutes lookin' around. What the hell was naggin' at me?

Stoney snorted impatiently.

I petted his neck. "I know, but just give me a minute. Somethin' don't seem right."

I drew my gun just in case, and walked into the cabin. The front lock had been smashed in, and there were obvious signs someone else had been through the place. It was a royal mess. All the pots and pans Kennedy's wife had spent a good portion of her life usin' to please her husband were gone, and mud tracks covered the floor. I looked into the second room, the one that had evidently just been added on recently. This was where the back door was located as well. It was obviously the new bedroom for the couple, and was complete with a crib and bed made of the same trees that the whole house had. And roughly. The construction of it all was sturdy, but not aesthetic in the least bit. I looked down at the basement, and realized that it must have been a major undertakin' in this rocky mountain to dig it. I looked up at the foundation walls, understandin' that most of the rocks excavated had been used for them.

Seein' there weren't nobody lurkin' to do me in, I holstered my gun and continued the self-guided tour. I descended the few rough steps into the cramped basement and looked around. I looked up, realizin' that only part of the cabin had been built on top of it. Looked like the kitchen portion. The rest of it was on bare ground that they had packed down, as was the normal thing to do. But this basement and its roof had been built sometime before the rest of it. Had Kennedy been plannin' a house here? Or had this been ruins from a previous occupant? I reckoned I'd never know for sure.

I looked around at the basement, seein' the now disturbed remains of the bodies I'd seen before. It looked like more the first time. As I took a closer look, there were maybe two people partially buried here. The skull I'd seen before was missin'.

"God damn looters," I said. That naggin' question in my mind wasn't answered down here, though. I climbed back up and looked around the cabin some more.

I found the remains of what looked like a secret compartment near where the bed was. Probably Kennedy's stash, already looted. Otherwise, the house looked and smelled like death. The whole thing was dark, and not just from the lack of light from outside. It lacked spirit. Kennedy had broken his wife's spirit here. I felt it.

I sighed in frustration and walked back out, Stoney with his ears up lookin' right at me. He whinnied.

"I'm a comin', damned impatient horse." I made my way to him and realized I'd better empty my bladder before the long ride back to E-Town. I looked up for a likely place to lay down some warm liquid, when the question that had been buggin' me suddenly answered itself. I looked around, and then around again. I looked into the woods, squintin' my eyes to see for sure. "Nah, that can't be right." I walked off to a nearby tree and relieved myself, continuin' to look around incredulously. I couldn't see it anywhere. "But, how can that be with a woman and a child in the house, and folks comin' by?" I asked. Nobody answered but Stoney with another impatient snort.

I finished up waterin' the tree and took another quick walk around, this time from the door of the cabin, walkin' the most logical direction I could think of, one that would be downwind of the cabin durin' summer. About a good twenty yards out, I stopped and looked around. Nope. Nothin'. Of course in the snow covered ground I couldn't be sure there hadn't been one and maybe it'd been knocked down, but... no. The snow wasn't that deep. In any case, I woulda fallen into the hole left behind. There should have been some kinda sign of one.

"Why in tarnation would you build such an elaborate cabin, with a corral and stable, especially expectin' regular payin' customers, and not have a damn outhouse?"

Nobody answered.

I jogged back to the cabin and looked around inside again. There, next to the bed, was an obvious round indentation in the dirt floor that I hadn't paid mind to before. "A commode?" I asked. "A damned chamber pot? That's all?" I looked around for it, and it was missin' too. I reckoned the looters had taken *all* the pots. There was a similar indentation near the roughly built fireplace in the larger room. So, Kennedy didn't care much about personal hygiene and all, fine with lettin' folks shit in a bucket, when a simple outhouse would have been easy enough to build. I shook my head. What a miserable life this woman had led. I gazed at the pieces of flesh still stuck on the fireplace stones. "What a bastard," I said. "Maybe I *shoulda* shot him in the woods instead of bringin' him in."

By the time I got back to E-Town, the snow fall had eased up, thankfully. But there were heavy clouds threatenin' to descend from the north. This was nothin' but a lull. I looked at Moreno Valley as I returned, amazed at how big E-Town had grown. There must have been near five thousand or more people crammed in there. I remembered readin' an issue of the *Elizabeth Lantern,* the local newspaper, that there would likely be more than ten thousand in Moreno Valley by the end of 1871 if the gold held out.

I stopped Stoney and counted buildin's as I approached the town. There were too many to count, upwards of a hundred or more. I counted six stores includin' Moore's, Middaugh's which was behind their saloon, and the drug store. There were seven saloons, three dance halls, the two hotels, Mutz and Lambert of course, the E-Town brewery, the flour depot, the sawmill, a schoolhouse, the livery, and the slaughterhouse. Not to mention the cabins and tents all over the place. Of course, we'll not mention the 'places of pleasure.' And, oh. Two churches, 'cause even in a town this size folks couldn't decide on how to worship God after they'd been drunk and paid for some female companionship. I chuckled and urged Stoney along.

I made it to the livery, and there was Jeff workin' on somebody's horseshoes, the forge blazin' and heatin' up the stables real nice. I led Stoney to his stall and got him settled in. I took off the saddle and such, and then began brushin' him down as Jeff brought over a fresh pile of hay and some oats, settin' them in the feed trough.

"There's fresh water under that layer of ice," he said as he pointed to the bucket in Stoney's stall. "Just punch it through. It's pretty thin with all the heat in here."

I did so, and sure enough. Water bubbled up, and Stoney drank his fill.

"So, you find him?" Jeff asked.

"No, he wasn't there. He'd been there recently, though. The fireplace was warm."

"Too bad. Sorry that was a wasted trip, Mike."

"Nah, it wasn't. Any time out ridin' Stoney is time well spent," I said as I brushed him.

"You sure do love that horse."

"Horses are pure, Jeff. They love and live with honor and loyalty, if they're shown that in return. You know he was never green broke?"

"Really?"

I nodded. "I just raised him with kindness, and he's shown me nothin' but the same all his life. There have been many times in my life I'd rather spent my time out on the range with nobody but him. Humans let you down. They're cruel and selfish. Greedy."

Jeff nodded and went back to his chores. "Can't argue with you there."

But there were certain humans I did like. My friends Clay and Davy, and a few others. The Daniels family back in Texas. And of course, Miss Carmen. That night I spent with her, apologetic about forgettin' her dishes again. Dangit. I'd have to pay her another visit later.

Chapter 5

The next mornin' was greeted by fresh coffee, with my breakfast in bed, a beautiful woman, and snow outside on the ground. Carmen lay next to me smilin' like she always did when I stayed with her. I reckon she smiled this time mostly 'cause of the bath she'd given me the night before.

"So, when are you going to make an honest woman out of me, Mike Austin?" she asked.

I chewed my food and considered her question. I looked around at the fine accommodations, the lace over the windows and all, the clean sweet smells. "A feller could get used to this kinda life. I can see it happenin' easy."

"Well?"

There was a knock on the door.

"Miss Carmen? There's a man looking for Mister Austin." It was one of her girls.

"Who is it?" I asked. "Damn annoyin' time of the mornin' to come callin'."

"He says he's Charles Kennedy's lawyer, a Mister Mills."

There went my appetite. "That piece of shit got a lawyer already?" I said quietly to Carmen. "How's that possible?"

"News travels fast," Carmen said.

"Tell him I'll be right there," I said. "To give him a piece of my mind," I said quietly.

"Mike, be nice. Remember what happened last time you lost your temper around a law man."

I nodded and gritted my teeth as I got up and got dressed. "He deserved what he got."

Moments later I stood in front of a dandy. He stood about a foot shorter than me, with short hair parted in the middle, a high-dollar suit on, and pasty skin. He smiled at me with pearly white, perfect teeth. Teeth I suddenly wanted to loosen with a nice knuckle sandwich. He put out his hand.

"Mister Austin, Melvin Mills, attorney for Mister Charles Kennedy."

I looked down at his hand, and then up into his light brown eyes. "So?"

"I'd like to ask you a few questions about the night you abducted Mister Kennedy."

"Abducted?"

"Yes, sir, if you wouldn't mind."

"I suppose it's a free country."

"Could we go somewhere… more private?"

"I'm headed to Pearson's. You can ask all you want while I walk, but you'd better not get me into a foul mood this early in the mornin'." I grabbed my hat, slammed it on my head, and checked my revolver. I made sure the caps were good, rotatin' the cylinder around a click at a time. I glared up at him. "Folks don't tend to like me much when I'm in a foul mood." I slid it in the holster, winked at Carmen, and exited her fine establishment. Mister Mills hesitantly followed me out.

It was damn cold outside. I could tell that by the way folks were actin'. Everyone wearin' coats and such. Sure, I could feel it too, but it wasn't anywhere near the kinda cold I'd felt before. I realized that I should probably get mine from my rig at the Livery at some point. It was an uncomfortable temperature outside to be sure. The snow crunched under our boots as we walked, and the clear blue sky with the sun shinin' on it made me think of home again. I took a deep breath of the crisp air, wonderin' when the next storm would blast through. I glanced to the north, seein' the dark clouds already buildin'. It wouldn't be long.

The lawyer started talkin', but I ignored him for the most part. I had my own agenda. I figured I'd mosey over to Pearson's where the whiskey would be nice and warm like the wood stove.

"Mister Austin, did you hear me?" Mills asked.

"Nope."

"I said, did you personally take Mister Kennedy into custody along with the illegal posse of twenty men led by Clay Allison? And did you personally beat him within an inch of his life, before Mister Allison drug him thirty miles to Elizabethtown?"

I spun around on my heels, ready to punch him out right there. Instead, I poked his chest with my finger, pushin' him back a bit. "Mister, you need to get your facts straight before you go accusin' folks of shit. Talk like that can cause a feller to disappear."

He put up his hands in defense. "Now, Mister Austin. There's no need for threats. I'm just asking you what's already been reported." He reached into his vest, causin' me to flinch. He cautiously pulled out a portion of the newspaper, where it as much as said that very thing.

I grabbed and read it.

"So, you can read?"

"Of course I can read." I crumbled up the paper and dropped it. "So, lawyers get their defense strategies from the newspaper now, huh?"

"You're saying it's not true?"

I stepped toward him, causin' him to step back. "Three of us apprehended a dangerous criminal, who offered no resistance, and brought him to justice. That's all."

"Three, not twenty?"

"No."

"Who was leading this illegal hunting posse?"

"It wasn't a posse. It was just three law-abidin' citizens escortin' a man to jail to face justice. That's all."

"And who were these other men?"

"None of your god damn business," I said through gritted teeth. I spun around and continued toward the saloon.

"Mister Austin, I have it on good authority it was David Crockett and Clay Allison leading this mob. You will be asked this on the stand, you might as well say so now."

"On the stand? You plannin' to call me to testify, Mister fancy lawyer? Then let me tell you somethin'. That piece of shit you're representin' killed *his own son*, a little boy of no more than three years old who didn't do nothin' to deserve it. He was just a boy, for God's sake! He also killed a good friend of mine who had a wife and child back home. He's killed who knows how many, and beat the hell out of his wife." I stepped toward him again, pushin' him back with my chest. "As far as I'm concerned, any son of a bitch who represents a man like Charles Kennedy is no better than him. Now leave me be!"

He fell on his ass. "Oh, you will be called, Mister Austin. Count on that!"

"Good. While you're at it, call all them people he's had dealin's with over the years, and hey, here's an idea. Call all the ones he's buried under his house! Oh, that's right, you can't, 'cause they're dead!" I turned around and saw Clay standin' out front of the saloon, along with a bunch of other fellers. I glanced around, and it turned out we'd had an audience. I saw a good dozen folks or more watchin' the conversation. I shook it off and walked into the saloon, Clay pattin' me on the back.

"I told him the same thing, Mike," Clay said. "He's just a fancy lawyer paid with all the gold Kennedy's stolen from his clients over the years. Don't worry about it. He'll get his due."

I bellied up to the bar. "John, I'm buyin' a bottle of your fancy whiskey."

John, the bartender and owner of this saloon, was a nice lookin' feller who everyone respected, 'cause he never judged. He just did his job, and listened. "Sure, Mike. How fancy we talking about?"

"Just give me some of that Tennessee Sour Mash." I dropped a twenty dollar coin on the bar.

"How many glasses?"

I looked at Clay, a group of men around him watchin' like they had designs on sharin' a drink with us. God damn vultures. I shook my head and looked back at Clay. "Two glasses *only.*"

The spectators gave a collective sigh and began to disburse.

He set us up, and Clay sat next to me. "A bit early for whiskey ain't it, partner?"

"That damn lawyer got me all riled up, Clay." I looked over at him. "What're you doin' back here? I thought you went back to the ranch."

"Oh, there's some stuff going on with folks trying to charge rent to folks who don't own the land they're on. It's all 'cause of Maxwell selling the land grant. I just needed to make sure we were all good on that. Then, I decided to come on back and make sure Kennedy hanged one way or another."

"The Maxwell Grant. I've been hearin' a lot about that lately," I grumbled out. "I heard he came out smellin' like a damn rose on that deal."

"That he did. More than a million dollars from what I hear." He shook his head. "Leaving the rest of us holding the bag."

John put the opened bottle of whiskey on the bar, along with two glasses. He took my money. "You want a beer to chase that down, gentlemen?"

I shook my head.

"Sure," Clay said. He tossed a coin on the bar.

"Put it on my tab," I said.

"Mike, you don't have to do that," Clay said.

"I'm thinkin' of goin' home, Clay," I said. "Back to Augusta."

"Homesick, huh?"

I nodded. "I ain't been back since just after the war." I poured him and me full glasses. "There weren't much left of the plantation. The main house was burned to the ground, and all the crops were ruined. The livestock had been stolen. All my family were killed." I paused for a moment as terrible memories flashed through my mind. Memories of burnt bodies. My parents, my young siblings. The woman I'd planned to marry some day from the neighborin' plantation. I had to bury them all. I struggled to push the memories and the buildin' tears away.

Clay patted my back.

"Maybe I could go back and make a go of it," I said. "Claim my land and… I don't know." I shook my head, suddenly realizin' I didn't feel as strongly as I had about goin' home before speakin' up about it. Once I heard it out loud, all I felt was profound sadness, not homesickness.

"Been feeling that way about Tennessee, to be honest." He lifted his glass. "To Dixie, my friend."

"Old times there are not forgotten," I said, grimly.

We tapped our glasses together and drank them down.

Smooth.

John sat the beer on the bar just as we finished, and Clay sipped on it. The two of us sat silent for a few moments, each of us lost in memories.

"What about that ranch out in Agua Dulce you been talking about, Mike? The one Captain Daniels runs?"

I chuckled. "The other Clay in my life. Yeah, I owe them a visit too."

"I'd hate to see you go, Mike. You're about the only other feller besides Davy who sees things the way I do around here."

I glanced around the full saloon. "Oh, I doubt that. Where *is* Davy?"

"I don't know. He said something about business down south. He left Cimarron yesterday." He chuckled. "We got a bit rowdy when we got back from here."

"Rode that horse into a saloon again?"

He smirked. "Maybe. A little bit." He sipped on his beer.

"So, I reckon it'll be just you and me testifyin', then."

"Word is, they're bringin' in Jose Cortez- that drifter from Taos Pass, a doctor who they sent to go look at the bodies, and some other fellers. I guess Justice McBride's going to do some sort of pre-trial hearing today."

"Today? Damn that's quick. Maybe we can see Kennedy hang before dinner," I said in a chuckle. I poured us another glass.

"I wouldn't count on it, Mike. Kennedy's got that lawyer now. I have no idea how he got the word so quickly, but one thing's for sure. This is going to be a high profile case. I'm beginning to wonder if we done the right thing by bringing him in."

"I was out lookin' for Jose, couldn't find him. Kennedy probably killed him too. We should've hanged him," I said. I shook my head. "Damn it, we should've just strung that bastard up right there where we found him."

"See? You shoulda listened to me."

"Which time, Clay? When you wanted to bring him in, or when you decided you wanted him hanged?"

He scowled at me. "You really are a foul person sometimes, Mike."

"Just, some things about this have really been gettin' to me. I went back out there, to Kennedy's place."

"Yeah?"

"Yeah. Clay, he built a two room cabin with a kitchen, and a basement."

"I remember, so?"

"He had a decent sized corral that could hold in a small herd of horses and mules, and even a stable. Of course, they weren't the best constructed, but sturdy enough."

"He was running a way station, so that don't sound too unusual. What's eating at you, Mike?"

83

"Clay, don't you think, with all that, plus a wife and child, and folks droppin' by on a regular basis, he shoulda built an outhouse?"

Clay paused, the look of bewilderment on his face. "Wait, he had to have one, surely."

I shook my head. "Nope. I looked around, too."

"Maybe the wind knocked it down."

"That don't seem likely, Clay. With the rough but sturdy construction of everythin' else he put up, why would he skimp on such an important buildin'?"

"Oh, come on, now. Everyone knows that's the first thing you build." Clay sipped his beer. "You gotta have a pot to shit in before anything else."

"That's just my point. He had one, maybe two. Commodes, I mean. But no outhouse. Don't you think with a woman and a child that it would be a priority?"

"Okay, so no outhouse. So, it wasn't important. So what?"

"It's just one more thing that sticks in my craw, Clay. He didn't give a damn about that woman or the boy, and less about his patrons. It was all about gettin' them in there to get their money. It just shows how low he is, and why we shoulda killed him when we had the chance."

"You the boys who brought him in?" Some feller just a bit older than us said as he staggered up to us, drunk and it wasn't even noon. He was a lanky feller with long brown hair that had streaks of grey in it. He wore a dusty blue US Cavalry hat, and had a prominent scar on his cheek.

"Yes, sir," Clay said.

"He killed my son Taylor. He was headed down the mountain with his minin' results. Done cashed in, and Kennedy killed him. Took all he had. You shoulda just strung him up! Don't you know he's gonna be released?! Leave it to goddamn Johnny Rebs to fuck it up."

Clay and I looked at each other, and shook our heads. A fight was not what we needed right now. But, to be honest, it sure would take the edge off.

"What's a matter, Johnny Rebs?! Can't handle a low down murderin' son of The South like you two? Is that why you didn't handle it? 'Cause you're baby murderers just like him? Is he your buddy?!"

"Sir, I'd advise you to step back," Clay said. "This ain't a conversation you should be having right now, considering your inebriated state."

"Oh, what's that? Tennessee accent? Just like your buddy Kennedy, huh? Both low down Johnny Rebs from Tennessee. Probably neighbors, huh? All them damn fancy soundin' words and all, but you don't have what it takes to deal out justice, huh? No wonder The South surrendered, you ain't got the guts. You're just a yellow bellied sap sucker, ain't ya'?"

I stood up, but then I caught the eye of John, who was holdin' his sawed-off shotgun behind the bar. He shook his head.

Clay took off his hat and scratched his head. "You best back away, sir." He popped his hat back on and grimaced at the northerner. "Before you say something you'll regret."

"Take it outside, boys," John said.

The entire population of the saloon suddenly took notice. Several patrons decided it was gettin' too rough, and exited the place like it was burnin'.

I looked at Clay, and he nodded. We both took one more drink of whiskey and walked out into the snow.

The northerner watched us leave, and started laughin'. "Typical. Damn cowards."

"Come on outside and say that," I said.

His smile faded. "I believe I will." He staggered out behind us.

"I got this," Clay said to me. "You just stand back." He took off his hat and scratched his head.

"Don't kill him, Clay. He said Kennedy killed his son. He's a witness."

"I said I got this." He frowned at me.

I put up my hands in defense, and backed away.

"God damn Johnny Reb bastards!" he said. "I oughta just kill you right here!" He drew his gun, nice and sloppy.

I didn't see Clay shoot, but I heard it. Damn fast, he was.

The northerner's gun went flyin', and he staggered back with shock on his face. "You... you shot my gun!"

"Now look here, Mister!" Clay said with fire in his eyes. "You said Kennedy killed your son. That means you're a witness. That means you deserve to live. *For now.* But the next time you draw on me, you won't be so lucky, understand?!"

The northerner fell to his knees, clutchin' his bleedin' hand. It was only grazed, but must 'ave hurt like hell. "He was only twenty years old. Twenty! My wife Anna died in childbirth. He was my only child, and Kennedy killed him!"

Clay sighed, lettin' his temper cool down. He knelt down and offered the northerner a rag for his hand. "Come on, let's put all this war time nonsense behind us for now. Let me buy you a drink, Mister...?"

"Sanders. Brian Sanders." He took Clay's hand and stood up. "You coulda killed me. You had me dead to rights."

Clay helped wrap Brian's hand. "And the next time you draw on me, I will."

Brian nodded. He looked down at his hand and back at his busted revolver as it slowly sunk into the snow. "I don't reckon I'll be drawin' on anyone for a while."

"That's a good thing," Clay said.

Now, that weren't the first time I seen Clay spare a feller's life, but every time he did so, it always gave me a surprise. But, truly, the feller didn't deserve to get killed. Not today.

We went back inside, and true to 'Gentlemen' Clay's word, he bought Brian a drink. Coffee.

"Coffee?" Brian said. "What about whiskey, or beer?"

Clay patted him on the back. "You need to slow down a bit. Pace yourself. Besides, we need to talk about Kennedy."

"Good idea," Deputy Houx said as he walked in. "Boys, I need you at the jail. Justice McBride needs your statements."

"But we already told you what happened," I said.

He sighed. "It's not just him. Kennedy's lawyer is there. This is the pre-trial hearing."

"We already talked to that lawyer," Clay said. "He harassed Mike on the way in. What more could that sack of shit lawyer want?"

"We have to do this right, boys. Come on," Deputy Houx said.

Brian stood up. "Then I'm goin' too. That son of a bitch killed my son."

Several other men stood up and joined us, ready for action one way or 'nother.

"Hold your horses, boys," Deputy Houx said. "This is just a hearing. Justice McBride wants to get some things on record before he makes a decision to hold over for a grand jury."

"Grand jury?" I said. "Are you serious? This is cut and dry! He killed them folks! He needs to hang, god damn it!"

He glared at me for usin' my foul language. "Mike, don't you go gettin' your bloomers in an uproar!" He pointed at me. "And the rest of you, calm down! The last thing we need is an angry mob, understand?!"

"So, where's the Sheriff?" Clay asked. "Shouldn't he be here?"

"There's something going on up north, I don't know the details. Come on, let's go."

Everyone began to move.

"Just Mike and Clay!" he said. "The rest of you just cool your damn heels!"

Arguments and shouts of anger came from the crowd, but they stayed as we walked out.

"Where's Davy?" Houx asked. "Justice McBride asked for him too."

"He left town on business," Clay said.

"Typical. Going to shoot up another saloon, no doubt."

I chuckled. "Probably."

A few minutes later we walked into a crowded jail house. Justice McBride sat at the deputy's desk siftin' through papers. Mister Mills stood next to Kennedy, who stood up holdin' onto the bars. I saw Carmen's plates stacked up on the floor next to the desk. I needed to get them back to her. The number of plates had doubled, so I guessed she'd taken on the task of feedin' the murderer. Too bad she didn't slip in some poison. On the other side of the jail house was Doctor Westerling. He nodded at me. He and I shared Norwegian heritage, and we'd talked about family history a time or two while he bandaged me up for one thing or another.

"Doc," I said.

"Mister Austin," he said with his thick accent. "Good to see you. No more gunshot wounds?"

"No, not today."

"Let's try to keep it that way, shall we?" He grinned through his ridiculously long mustache.

"Gentlemen," McBride said. "I take it you all know each other already, so let's just get down to it. Where is Mister Crockett?"

"He's out of town," Clay said.

McBride nodded and pulled out a Holy Bible from his carpet bag, placin' it on the desk. "All of you raise your right hand and repeat after me. In the testimony I'm about to give, I swear to tell the truth, the whole truth, and nothing but the truth, so help me God."

We did as charged.

"For the record, we are in Deputy Houx's office, and he's in attendance and has already given his sworn written statement already on record. We have in custody the defendant Charles Kennedy, who has been accused of murder. He's being represented by his lawyer Mister Mills. Doctor Westerling is here who will testify to the nature of the bodies found. Then we have Missus Kennedy's sworn written statement already on record, which I obtained earlier this morning. We also have you two gentlemen, who are witnesses after the fact. Let's proceed." He looked at Clay. "Sir, state your full name for the record."

Clay cleared his throat. "Yes, your Honor. My name is Robert Clay Allison. I just go by Clay."

McBride wrote it down. "Mister Allison, please tell me in your own words what transpired on the night you apprehended Mister Kennedy at his home."

"Objection, your Honor," Mills said. "Clearly my client was abducted."

"Over ruled, Mister Mills. This is just a preliminary hearing. You can save your arguments for trial, if this goes that far."

"Please make a note of the objection, your Honor."

Justice McBride nodded and scribbled in his notes. "It is so noted. Mister Allison, continue."

"Your Honor. On the day in question, my associates Mike Austin, Davy Crocket and myself were enjoying a day off in Pearson's saloon when Missus Kennedy stumbled in, cold and obviously beaten. She told us the story of what her husband had done, that he had killed their son and—"

"Objection, Your Honor. My client has not been proven to have committed these crimes."

"Mister Mills, objection over ruled. As I said before, this is just a hearing. Your objection is noted. Please continue, Mister Allison."

"Anyhow, so we decided to go apprehend this dangerous crimin—"

"Objection! Your Honor, please!" Mills insisted.

"Counselor, please hold your objections until I can at least get this story on paper!" Justice McBride said.

"Yes, your Honor."

"Mister Allison, continue."

"We decided to go ask Mister Kennedy to accompany us to this jail to explain in a proper legal manner, how his son and Mister Pritchett came to be dead while in his care." Clay smiled.

"Ask?!" Kennedy yelled. "You dragged me behind your horse 'till I was nearly dead, after shooting at me and breaking into my house!" He rubbed his sore neck.

"Mister Mills! Control your client!" McBride said. "Mister Allison, were you acting on Deputy Houx's authority when you brought Mister Kennedy in?"

"Yes," Deputy Houx said.

"No, your Honor," Clay said as he glared at Houx. "We did this as law-abiding citizens in full accordance, and we did it without the deputy's knowledge. We brought Mister Kennedy straight here and released him into the deputy's custody."

"Deputy Houx, you're saying they were acting under your authority?" McBride asked.

"Well, see, your Honor… once they brought him in, I told them they did the right thing."

"Deputy, there is no such thing as retroactive legal authority in this case."

"Yes, your Honor."

"Deputy Houx was drunk!" Kennedy blurted out. "He didn't know anything about it 'til I was nearly dead! Them bastards tried to kill me!"

"Mister Mills!" McBride yelled.

"That's callin' the kettle black," I said quietly. "Charley was so drunk he could hardly stand."

"I'm sorry, your Honor. It won't happen again." Mills and Kennedy began talkin' in heated whispers.

"Mister Austin, we'll get to you in a minute. Now, Mister Allison. What's all this about you breaking into Mister Kennedy's house?" McBride asked.

"Your Honor. When we arrived we smelled something decaying. The back door was open, and we decided there might be some trouble inside. Perhaps someone in need."

"Someone in need, huh?"

"Yes, your Honor."

"So, you went inside and apprehended Mister Kennedy?"

"That was me," I said. "He ran out the back and I ran to catch up with him."

"I said we'll get to you in a minute," McBride said to me again, a frown on his face. "Mister Allison, please continue."

"So, we entered the house and found what looked like human bones in the fireplace. We also saw signs of a fight, blood on the floor and on the fireplace stones. We followed the trail into the basement, where we found the bodies of a small boy and a man. Also, we found what looked like some partial skeletons, including a skull buried there."

"Continue."

"We then escorted Mister Kennedy to E-Town."

"Do you have anything further to add to this statement at this time, Mister Allison?"

"No, your Honor, that about sums it up."

"Thank you. Mister Austin, please state your full name for the record."

I cleared my throat and straightened my posture. "Michael Angelico Thurman Austin."

"Mister Austin, do you agree with Mister Allison's testimony as far as you were involved?"

"Yes, your Honor."

"Describe the part where you followed Mister Kennedy."

"Well, sir, he tore out the back, jumped on Mister Pritchett's horse, who I recognized. I ran after him on my horse, 'til Mister Kennedy decided to come along peacefully."

"He's lying!" Kennedy said.

McBride ignored him. "Mister Austin, did Mister Kennedy resist?"

"Not exactly resist, your Honor. He was pretty drunk and stumbled a bunch of times. We had to practically carry him back."

"They beat me up, Judge!" Kennedy yelled. "And then they drug me!"

"Mister Austin, please describe exactly how Mister Kennedy was escorted to E-Town."

"Well, your Honor, we let him walk to help sober him up. He was fallin' down everywhere, so we secured him with rope so he wouldn't hurt himself no more."

"So, you're saying you didn't drag him behind your horse?"

"Yes, your Honor. I didn't do no such thing."

"I see. So, you tied up Mister Kennedy, and he walked. Behind your horse, and he was drunk."

"My horse," Clay said. "I had him tied to my horse. Mike was ponying Pritchett's horse, with Mister Pritchett and the boy's body draped over."

"Mister Allison, Mister Austin. Thank you, gentlemen. That will be all for now. Please stay in the area in case I have more questions for you."

We nodded and began to leave.

"Your Honor, don't I get to cross examine?" Mills asked.

"Not today you don't."

"This is a travesty!" Mills said.

Clay and I exited, to the sounds of them still arguin'.

"Well, I feel pretty good about it," Clay said. "That Mills feller will try to make it look like we done something wrong, but you can see McBride knows better."

"I still think we should have hanged him. Somethin' don't feel right."

"Mike, Mike, Mike. You and your feelings. Let's go fix that right now. We got nearly a whole bottle of whiskey waiting for us."

I laughed. "I suppose you're right."

Chapter 6

The next day we were back on Clay's ranch. The weather was gettin' worse, and we had work to do. We rounded up all his cattle, only a handful missin', and put them in the big corral to wait out the storm. And it was goin' to be a big one. Rollin' dark clouds came over us, turnin' day to night and droppin' several feet of snow on us, along with some uncomfortable freezin' rain. We spent the time just dealin' with this. Feedin' the livestock, keepin' them alive, and keepin' warm as best we could. The Allisons' house was not much more than a cabin itself, as was the bunkhouse where I stayed with the boys. Clay asked me time and time again to come stay with him and his family, but they were already too crowded. At least in the bunkhouse I felt more at ease, not so pressured to put on airs, so to speak. Hell. I would have been fine to camp outside, but I knew that would be a bad idea, regardless of my tolerance to the cold. They'd find me all snuggled up in my bedroll frozen stiff. My grave marker would say somethin' about me preferin' the cold to people, I imagine.

Me and the boys spent the down time, once chores were done, playin' cards and just restin'. It was a hard life, but what the hell else was I goin' to do? I had that little claim up in the mountains, but I wasn't too eager to get back to it. We all but forgot about Kennedy 'til that evenin'.

The weather had let up some, and Clay came to the bunkhouse with a note in his hand. "Mike, we have to get back to E-Town."

"Hell of a time to say so, Clay. Cimarron pass is probably impossible to get through."

"No, not impossible. This came via currier." He handed me the note.

Oct 5 70
From: Dty Houx, ETown
To: Clay A, Mike A, Cim
Grand Jury on October 6 9AM U R summoned.

"They got court quick enough," I said. "Grand jury, huh?"

"Yep, we gotta be there, Mike. We gotta make this right. For that woman, for that boy. For your friend and all them that Kennedy killed."

"They probably ain't even got them in the ground yet, it bein' so cold." I shook my head. I suddenly felt the pull to El Paso again, to see Missus Pritchett. I'd have to wait 'till all this mess was over.

"I suspect not. Come on, get ready. We leave in half an hour." Clay left.

The sky had cleared up once again as we headed out through the deep snow. It was beautiful with all the snow drapin' over the trees, the moonlight lightin' our way, but it was also deadly to those not experienced. Stoney was not happy with the situation, but he'd been through worse. It was dark and cold out, though, and he was damn near ready to buck me off. I'd taken Águila back to the ranch with me, and considered saddlin' him up instead. But, no. Even in his cantankerous state, Stoney would hate me if I went somewhere without him. I patted his neck. "It ain't that far, boy. You'll be fine."

He snorted.

"So, when's the big occasion?" Clay asked.

"The what?"

"You obviously love that horse more than any woman I've ever seen you with, even Miss Carmen. So, when are you going to marry Stoney, make it official?" He laughed.

"Very funny, Clay."

Other than the few words here and there, we didn't talk much on our trip. It was a good fifty miles through the pass, in some normally nice ridin' when the weather was clear. But just after a little blizzard like we'd had, it took us all night to get through it. Our horses had to step high, even in the places that had already seen traffic. On this night, though, the only folks we seen were ourselves.

Just as the sky started to lighten from twilight, we arrived in Moreno Valley. We rode through Eagle Nest and into Elizabethtown to see it already bustlin' with folks as the new day dawned. We checked in at the livery.

Jeff was already up, doin' chores in a full stable. When he saw us ride in, he just shook his head. "Well, it's about time you got here."

"We just got the note last night," Clay said.

We looked around.

"Full stable," I said. "Can you do some musical stalls and get our horses some warm accommodations?"

He nodded. "Of course, but you boys need to get to Middaugh Saloon."

"Whiskey for breakfast?" I said.

"That's where they're havin' court," Jeff said. "It's the biggest open saloon in town, and the only place that'll accommodate everyone. They're already doin' jury selection."

"Jury selection. From E-Town? That could be interesting," Clay said.

"Yeah, finding an impartial group of folks will be a neat trick," Jeff said. "I'm headed over in a bit. You boys should get on over there."

We did.

The bustlin' town was that way for a reason, turned out. As we turned the corner toward Middaugh Saloon we saw what looked like all the citizens of E-Town crowdin' around, the entrance packed tighter'n a prospector's burro on his way to the mountains.

As we got closer we saw folks from not just E-Town, but some from further away. Some total strangers. But when they all saw us two makin' our way up there, they turned to us.

"That's them!" a familiar voice said. "That's Mike Austin and Clay Allison!" It was that feller Clay spanked, Brian. "Make way, folks! They're prime witnesses!" He began shovin' people out of the way 'til it looked like Moses at the Red Sea. They parted, creatin' a corridor right up to the entrance.

We nodded and said, "Thanks," and the classic, "Much obliged," and so forth 'till we were just inside the door. A hastily written sign on the door said, 'No guns allowed during proceedings.' It was a rare thing for me not to be wearin' a gun, but the law is the law, and all that. Clay and I reluctantly removed our belts and handed them to the attendant, a young boy of around ten years old wearin' a thick coat. He placed them in a box on the boardwalk. His eyes were wide as he looked up at us.

I tousled his hair, smiled, and we walked in.

Justice McBride sat at a table in the middle of the extra large dance floor all by his lonesome as a group of twenty presumably jurors sat at the bar. I didn't recognize any of them, but they looked no better'n a group of saddle tramps waitin' on some rot gut whiskey to warm 'em up. It was a silly scene, but seein' as E-Town was now the county seat and there hadn't been a town hall built yet, I suppose this was the biggest place to have this sort of thing.

"Hell of a venue for court," Clay said. "I wonder if we get a complimentary bottle of Jameson's for our testimony."

"That'd be alright, but I prefer good ole Tennessee Sour Mash."

We both chuckled.

Mister Mills was in the middle of some rant about the process, when Justice McBride sighed and shook his head, makin' notes. There was also a pretty young woman sittin' nearby writin' things down at another table. The rest of the saloon was full of spectators. I didn't see Kennedy or the deputy anywhere, but I did see Missus Kennedy sittin' with the spectators. A young man of around twenty sat near McBride.

Mister Mills stood. "…and furthermore, your Honor, we have no reason to believe that Mister

Johnson would not make a fine juror, given the previously stated objections." He sat down.

Justice McBride nodded. "Mister Anderson?"

A feller I didn't recognize stood up. By his attire and demeanor, I could tell right away this was another low down lawyer. "Your Honor, I have no objection to this juror."

Justice McBride sighed in relief. "Finally. Mister Johnson, if you would please go sit with the other jurors."

"Yes... sir, your Honor, sir." Johnson did as ordered.

"Now, then," McBride began, "since we finally have a grand jury, we will proceed if all the witnesses are present." He looked through his notes. "Mister Cortez."

I saw Jose's diminutive stature rise from the back of the room. "Si, I am here, your Honor."

That answered the question of Mister Cortez's whereabouts.

"Doctor Westerling."

He stood up, towerin' over the crowd. "I'm here, your Honor."

"Missus Kennedy."

"I'm here, your Honor."

"Mister Tolliver."

Will Tolliver, A nice lookin' younger man I recognized as one of the spectators when we apprehended Kennedy, stood up. He was the only citizen dressed in a suit. "Here, your Honor."

"Mister Crockett."

There was no answer. McBride continued, "Mister Sanders."

"Yes! your Honor, I'm here!" Brian yelled from the entrance.

"Charles Kennedy and Deputy Houx are accounted for... Mister Coleman has already given his statement in absentia." He looked through his papers. "Mister Austin."

"I'm here, your Honor."

"Mister Allison."

"Present and accounted for, your Honor," Clay said. He bowed like some kinda aristocrat from Europe.

I nudged him with a smirk on my face. "Show off."

He winked back.

"That's all I have on the witness list for this court." Justice McBride cleared his throat. "Let it be known, that this is a grand jury examination. Questions will be asked by the jury directly of the witnesses. Attorney Mills will be representing the defendant Mister Kennedy to answer any questions of him, and Attorney Anderson will be representing the Territory of New Mexico as prosecutor, and will be in charge during these proceedings. Each witness will be called in, in turn, and will be questioned and re-examined by the jury as they see fit. Neither attorney will have the right of procedural objection. Once this is finished, the jury will retire to deliberate whether Mister Kennedy should be indicted and this case should be heard in a regular court of law when it convenes in the spring, or if the evidence is not sufficient to proceed. Are there any questions about the proceedings today?"

"In the spring?" I said.

"Yes, Mister Austin. The regular circuit court is held in March," Justice McBride said.

"That's a hell of a long time to keep Kennedy locked up," Clay said.

"Who's gonna pay for his upkeep?" Brian asked. "Us?"

The crowd began to get loud, realizin' the situation if Kennedy was kept.

"So, we're supposed to feed this murderer 'till March, is that what you're saying?" Clay asked. "You can't be serious."

"This is not a discussion for the grand jury," McBride said.

"The hell it ain't," I said. "You're sayin' that if, and only if, he's indicted, he'll be held in the jail for the next half a year? And what if he's let free? Has anyone considered the welfare of Missus Kennedy if he gets out? And what about bail?"

Maria was visibly shaken, tears of terror runnin' down her face.

McBride slammed his rickety gavel down. "This is not a matter for today!"

"Your Honor, clearly you can see that public opinion has corrupted these proceedings. I move to strike all the comments coming from the public," Mills said. "Further, I move that a new grand jury be picked, as they are now clearly swayed and no longer impartial."

"Denied!" McBride yelled. "Are the members of the grand jury clear on their duties?"

They all responded, "Yes." The newest one was busy lookin' through some sort of legal manual.

"Very well. The…" Justice McBride looked around at the saloon and shook his head. "The *court* will now be cleared of everyone but the attorneys and the grand jury. Mister Anderson, the court is yours."

Everyone stood around, wonderin' what to do next.

"Come on, let's go!" McBride said. He got up as well, shooing with his hands. "Get out, everyone… *now!*"

Anderson followed behind as McBride and all the witnesses and spectators filed out into the snow covered street. He locked the door behind us.

McBride then began walkin' toward the jail house as the rest of us just stood around outside like a bunch of wallflowers waitin' to be asked to dance.

"So, what are we supposed to do out here in the cold?" Clay asked Justice McBride. "Pull our dicks out and play Yankee Doodle?"

He turned around. "Wait to be called, if you're a witness. Everyone else, go home. You'll be notified of the results as soon as I know." He looked at the newspaper editor, who I didn't see there at first. "I'll tell the newspaper, and then everyone will know." He turned and walked away.

"I didn't realize this was supposed to be secret," I said.

"Grand juries are," Clay said. "He was just there to get it all up and running."

"Dios mio," Missus Kennedy said. "How long will we wait out here?" She looked up at the jail house. "Will... they call... *him?*" She was obviously terrified. She shivered from either the cold or terror. Probably both. "Will he be let out?"

Clay turned to her. "We'll protect you, Ma'am. He ain't getting anywhere near you."

"Damn right," I said.

The gathered crowd agreed.

She smiled at us. "You're angels."

I looked at Clay. "Hey, that's my middle name."

He chuckled. "Smart ass."

Carmen made her way through the crowd and right up to me. "Mister Austin, I'm running out of dishes."

I suddenly felt my cheeks burn. "Miss Carmen... I... er..."

"You forgot, didn't you?"

"Well..." I removed my hat. "I had to get back to Cimarron, do some chores for Clay..."

She put her arm around me and snuggled up. "Sure, sure."

I looked up at Clay, and he was grinnin' like the cat who done caught the canary.

"Shut up, Clay," I said with a frown.

He put up his hands. "I didn't say a word."

Carmen stretched up and kissed me. "You're so handsome. Come see me after this is over. Help me clean dishes." She grinned and walked away.

Clay chuckled. "Clean dishes. I bet."

I looked up at the crowd and saw Jose Cortez lookin' right at Missus Kennedy. She smiled at him with a warmth only a daughter could have. He nodded. Yep. I knew the truth, alright. Truth that could throw this whole case out of kilter. But my lips were sealed. I suddenly realized how she had made it all the way from her cabin to the saloon in E-Town. She'd had help. Jose had brought her to us, knowin' we'd help. He then looked up at me, his eyes fixed on mine with a desperate plea in them. I smiled and nodded, lettin' him know without a word that nobody would know what I did. His gaze eased.

Mister Anderson opened the door and said, "Mister Cortez."

Jose's demeanor suddenly changed from that of relief to that of extreme apprehension. "I'm coming." He disappeared into the saloon.

"This ain't right," I said. "No real court 'till March." I looked at Missus Kennedy. "Ain't right at all."

Clay nodded. "It ain't gonna happen, Mike. There's no damn way E-Town's gonna host that no-good..." He looked at Missus Kennedy. "It ain't gonna happen."

"You're damn right it ain't." I glared up at the jail house.

As the day dragged on, the temperature risin' a bit and some of the crowd slowly dispersin', our crew from Cimarron showed up, Clay's brother John leadin'. Jose had been in there for nearly two hours. Missus Kennedy as well as everyone else was gettin' worried.

"Clay," his brother John said as he rode up. He was obviously Clay's brother, a strong family resemblance. I'd say that John was probably a bit more even tempered than Clay, though. "We need you back home, Clay. Some feller's trying to claim we don't have rights on our own land. There's going to be trouble."

Clay took off his hat and scratched his head. "Damn it, I don't have time for this shit!" He shook his head. "I knew this was going to happen. Damn lawyers and businessmen putting their hands in everything. Did you show them the deed?"

109

"I did, said it ain't valid," John said. "They said they'd be back."

"It's happening all over," Brian said. "Since the Maxwell Grant was sold off."

"A war's comin'," I said.

Jose finally walked out, a look of defeat on his face. He wiped away tears and found Missus Kennedy in the crowd. He shook his head and walked down the street alone.

"Ah, shit," Clay said. "What the hell happened now?"

"Dios mio!" Missus Kennedy did the sign of the cross, tears rollin' down her face.

"Doctor Westerling," Anderson said. "You're up, Doctor."

Doctor Westerling made his way through the crowd and disappeared into the saloon.

"Clay, we have to go," John insisted.

"Just, wait, damn it!" Clay said. "This is important!"

John dismounted and rushed up to Clay. "We're going to lose it, Clay! We need you there to help, don't you get it?!"

Clay pushed John back. "Damn it, don't you get it?! This demon murdered his own kin! He has to pay for what he did!"

"He's bein' called as a witness, John," I explained. "He can't go 'till then."

John stepped back. "Jesus. Why is it when something bad happens, you just have to be right in the middle of it? Both of you!"

"Because, John. There has to be justice, order, or chaos will prevail," Clay said.

"This looks pretty damn chaotic to me," John said. "And you two, I've seen you two do some pretty damned chaotic shit. And you talk about law and order. You want justice? Let the law handle this matter and you two come back before they take our land. If we don't fight, there will be chaos, alright. And we'll be broke and homeless."

"You rode all this way just to yell at me?" Clay asked as he put his hat back on.

"No. There was a meeting in Eagle Nest that you missed because of this."

"You go on back, John. I ain't going nowhere until this is resolved. Then we'll both be back with guns loaded."

John fumed. "Typical. Gentleman Clay." He shook his head, jumped back on his horse, and the crew rode off.

Clay smiled at me. "See, he called me a gentleman."

"This shit about the land grant sounds serious," I said.

"Nah. We're locked in. There's no way anyone could take away what we already bought and paid for. They want to deny the deed, let 'em. They'll leave with a bullet between their eyes."

Doctor Westerling walked out, after only bein' in there for a few minutes. He shook his head.

"Missus Kennedy," Anderson said.

She gasped and looked at us. "I... can't do this!"

Clay took her hand in his and looked deep into her eyes. "Maria. You're a strong woman, stronger than you know. All you have to do is tell the truth. You have nothing to hide. They will ask you some uncomfortable questions, but it don't matter. Just tell the God's honest truth. All of it, like you told us. God's with you. We're all with you."

"Missus Kennedy?" Anderson asked again.

"Hold your god damn horses," I said. "She's a comin'."

Missus Kennedy wiped away her tears, nodded, and disappeared inside.

"Christ. She's a mess," Clay said. "They're gonna trip her up, I know it."

"It's just the jury askin' questions ain't it?"

"Sure, but still. I've got a bad feeling." Clay looked up at the jail. "Something don't feel right, Mike."

"That's what I've been sayin' all along."

"You're right," Doctor Westerling said. "I'm not sure that jury is all... genuine."

"Ah, hell," I said.

"What did they ask you?" Clay asked.

As soon as he said this, the crowd pulled in, gatherin' near.

"Just a few questions, but I'm not supposed to say," he said.

Everyone sighed and started talkin' about how much bullshit this was.

"But I don't give a shit," he said. "They asked me if what I found during my examination of the Kennedy house was for sure human bones. I said yes, obviously. Then they asked me to describe the cause of death, and obviously I didn't know, given the short time I had to examine the remains. Then they asked me what the causes of death were for Samuel Kennedy and Mister Pritchett. Since they hadn't been buried yet, I told them. Mister Pritchett had been shot in the head, and the boy had been beaten, his head crushed by a blunt object, probably the fireplace. Then…" he shook his head. "Then they asked me if I could tell who had committed these acts, purely from what I had seen from the remains." He lowered his head and shook it.

"Well?" Brian asked.

"How could I? No, I said, that could not be determined. It could have been anyone."

"Fuck," I said.

"Son of a bitch," Clay said.

"Holy shit," Brian said.

Doctor Westerling continued. "It's mostly a couple of them asking the questions. The others just sit and watch."

"The damn jury's been compromised," Brian said. "Paid off by Kennedy himself, no doubt."

"Now, we don't know that for sure," Doctor Westerling said. "Those are legitimate questions."

"Bullshit," Clay said. "Those are clearly leading questions, meant to point the blame away from Kennedy." He took off his hat and scratched his head. He looked at me. "We should have hung him when we had the chance."

All I could do was nod in agreement.

"Let's go do it now," Brian said. "To hell with this. We know he's guilty!"

Several voices in the crowd agreed.

"Just relax," Clay said. "Now's not the time for a damned angry mob. Let's let this grand jury show their hand. If it is corrupt, and we know this for sure, then McBride will order it invalid. Kennedy will get his comeuppance one way or another."

I nodded and thought, 'Oh, he will, alright.'

Clay looked at me as if I'd spoken this out loud. "And you just hold your damn horses, Mike. This is the kind of shit that can get out of hand real quick. Remember what happened last time."

"That son of a bitch got what he deserved, though."

"Sure, but the whole damn town didn't need to be burned down for it."

"Well... maybe not..."

Although the air temperature continued to rise, it didn't rise as much as the anger of folks outside as we waited for Missus Kennedy to emerge. Two hours passed, and it was already noon. Clay and I had to physically stop people from rushin' the jail as time passed.

Finally, just about one o'clock, Anderson emerged. "Break for lunch. We'll reconvene at two thirty."

We didn't see Missus Kennedy anywhere, nor the jury or Mister Mills.

"Where's Missus Kennedy?" I asked with teeth gritted.

"She's being sequestered until her testimony is finished," Anderson said.

"Mister Anderson, this is bullshit!" I argued. "What the hell's goin' on in there?!"

"The grand jury's compromised, ain't they?!" Brian yelled.

The crowd roared agreement.

Anderson put up his hands. "Please, listen!"

A few minutes passed as the crowd finally settled down.

"Missus Kennedy has been escorted by Mister Lambert, out the back, to her room. She's fine. The grand jury is remaining in the saloon for lunch. Mister Mills has also gone out the back, to Delah's Diner, where he'll be guarded. I suggest you all go home. You don't need to be here. All we need is the witnesses to reconvene here at two thirty."

"This is fixed, ain't it?!" Brian said. "Tell us!"

"Mister Sanders, and… all of you. I intend to prosecute Mister Kennedy to the full extent of the law. I have no doubt this grand jury will return with an indictment. Then I'll be able to cross examine him, and all you witnesses plus a few more I plan to call, and make damn sure he is found guilty! He will pay for his crimes!"

"Sure, in six god damn months! By then he'll be broke out of jail, and done killed…" I thought about Missus Kennedy. "Others."

"It won't be that long," Anderson said. "I've already prepared a motion for a special court session, to be held immediately after the grand jury."

"And what if it's denied?" Clay asked.

He shook his head. "It won't be. It's what's right for the case, for Kennedy to face justice now instead of being fattened up for half a year."

I nodded, satisfied that Anderson was at least tryin' to do the right thing.

"How do you know he did it?" a strange voice asked.

We all looked upon the face of Will Tolliver. "As far as I know, there is absolutely no real evidence *he* did any of this. It could have been Missus Kennedy for all we know. I mean, has anyone come forward and said they saw him do it?"

The crowd suddenly got loud.

"Sure, Jose did!" Jeff said from way in the back. "Didn't he?"

Anderson looked at him and slowly shook his head.

"Ah, shit," I said.

"We're about to lose control, partner," Clay said.

"I don't think we ever had it."

"Everyone, please!" Anderson yelled with his hands up. "Please!"

Several people pushed Will around, but he stood his ground.

"Now, listen to me very carefully!" Anderson began, "if this turns into a lynch mob, you'll all be charged with murder and meet your end on the gallows! Is that understood?!"

A few voices grumbled.

"This is not the time for vigilante justice! Let the system properly deal with this. All you're going to do is make things worse!"

"No," I said quietly to Clay. "The time for vigilante justice passed when we brought him in instead of hangin' him where we found him. I should have gone with my first instincts and shot that son of a bitch in the head."

"That's what I was trying to tell you then, as I recall," Clay said.

I looked him in the eye. "We just can't seem to get synchronized on our philosophy lately."

He nodded. "I noticed."

Chapter 7

Mister Anderson somehow managed to calm down the crowd, and most of them went home. Well, I honestly don't know where they went, but they disbursed. Clay, Brian, and I headed to The Broken Egg, a popular restaurant just a block away. It was a nice place that specialized in breakfast, and offered it all day long. I thought it was a strange concept, 'til the first time I had flapjacks and hash browns for dinner. Damn good. The restaurant itself was nothin' more than a rectangle buildin', the square dinin' area out front and the kitchen in back. The upstairs was the livin' quarters for the owners, a German couple who were about my age. They were a sweet couple, if I'm allowed to use that term. He mostly did the cookin', and she was the only waitress. They were both ample, if you catch my drift. We sat down in the crowded dinin' room and she was there right away to take our order.

"Guten Nachmittag," she said. "Would you like a few minutes to decide?" Her German accent was thick, to say the least.

The menus were already on the table.

"Actually, I'm ready," Clay said.

"Yeah, me too," I said.

"Starved. Let's get this show on the road," Brian said.

She stood ready to receive our orders. I realize it's probably of no consequence what we ordered, but just in case you need to know. I ordered scrambled eggs, hash browns, sausage, bacon, and toast. Black coffee. Clay ordered a chicken fried steak and eggs, also black coffee. Brian ordered biscuits and gravy, scrambled eggs. Also black coffee.

"Boys, I just want to say I'm sorry about all that Johnny Reb stuff last time," Brian said. "Clearly that war is over, and another is about to start. We need to be on the same side."

"Think nothing of it," Clay said. "And, I agree. It seems Colfax County could be on the verge of some kind of war."

"I thought you said it wouldn't happen," I said.

"I've been thinking about it since John showed up," Clay said. "We should be prepared for a hell of a fight."

Brian nodded. "Yeah, I agree."

"Well, I'm ready as you know, Clay. But... I do have somethin' I have to do down south first, after all this is done with Kennedy."

"Pritchett's wife, you mean."

"Yep. I need to take that horse to her, and let her know what happened, and where her husband is laid to rest. Of course, I won't go 'till that deed is done."

"Not going to try to take his body, huh?" Clay said.

"That's a long way to carry a body that's already been above ground a week. No."

"Wise decision."

"Speaking about Kennedy," Brian whispered. "How would you feel if just the three of us broke him out and stretched his neck?"

I shook my head. "I would love nothin' better, but I think that horse has already left the barn."

"We could wait 'till tonight, sneak him out, take him to the slaughterhouse. Hang him nice and clean from them high beams they use to hang beef for slaughter, then put him back in his cell. Nobody would know nothing."

"The deputy is there day and night now," I said. "His wife and Carmen are takin' turns feedin' them. Now with everyone else in town, I don't see how we could get away with it."

"Get away with it," Clay said as he shook his head. "I would just as soon drag his ass through town by his neck, show the world what happens to low-down pieces of shit around here. Get away with it? To hell with that. Nobody in this town with any kind of morals would say they saw a damn thing. You saw that crowd."

I leaned back in my chair. This made the most sense I'd heard yet. "So, instead of an angry lynchin' mob, just the three of us." I stroked my chin. "This could work. Don't make it about the mob, make it about good old fashioned justice. And don't try in the least to hide it. Make it public. We'd be untouchable."

Clay nodded. "As public as possible. That deputy wouldn't resist, and you damn well know it. If we just explain the situation to him, he'd back down sure as the sun rises."

"So, tonight?" Brian said.

"No," I said. "After the grand jury does its thing. In broad daylight. If they really are corrupt, there'll be a mob."

Clay chuckled. "And they'll have a hell of a time controlling it. But we won't be there. After our testimony we'll meet at the slaughterhouse and wait. That's close enough that we'll be able to see what's happening."

"Right," Brian said. "If there's a cheer, then it went right. We can relax and let the law hang the bastard. But if they protest, we'll know what to do."

"I'm inclined to say we should do this either way," I said. "If even one of them jury members was paid off, and even if they do indict, we could still see an acquittal durin' a formal trial. If

Anderson can get a quick trial like he said. Otherwise, we're lookin' a long winter."

"I'm impressed you know that much about the law, Mike," Clay said with a smirk. "Being Sheriff of Stanton taught you a thing or two, huh?"

I chuckled. "Sheriff, for like a minute. But, nah. I was gonna learn this stuff a long time ago, but only got through a few books."

"So," Brian began. "You're saying we should hang the bastard in any case."

"Just wait," Clay said. "If it does go that far, and he is declared not guilty, we'll just make sure he has a fatal accident on his way home." He grinned.

I shook my head. "No. It ain't enough. The world needs to know. I mean, we could just go ahead and hang him from a visible place, and leave him there with a sign hangin' from his neck sayin' this is what happens to baby murderers around here. That might do."

Brian chuckled. "I kind of like that."

"Here we are, plotting vigilante justice with a damn Yankee as our cohort," Clay said in a chuckle.

"Here I am, plotting justice with a couple of Johnny Rebs," Brian said.

"What's the world comin' too?" I said.

We all chuckled.

Everyone was back at the saloon as the time came, includin' pretty much the entire town. It was more crowded than before.

Anderson came out. "We're about to reconvene. As soon as Missus Kennedy is finished with her testimony, which..." he sighed. "Honestly, I don't see how this could result in anything but an indictment. Poor woman. All she's gone through... anyway, after she testifies and if it ain't too late in the day, the rest of the witnesses will be called." He retreated back into the saloon.

"If it ain't too late?" I said. "What the hell else do they have to do? Plan a barn dance?"

"That's bullshit," Clay said.

"Plan A?" Brian said.

"Just keep it quiet," Clay said. "Let this play out."

Minutes turned to hours, and the crowd began to disburse again. Seemed folks were gettin' tired of waitin'.

Missus Kennedy finally came out just ahead of Anderson. It was fairly obvious he'd been moved, his eyes showin' signs of tears shed. She cried and ran into my arms, cryin' heavily.

"Mister Tolliver," Anderson called. "You're up, sir."

We all looked in surprise that he was still alive, and not strung up himself for supportin' Kennedy. He straightened his tie and disappeared into the saloon.

"Jesus," Clay said.

"Missus... Maria," I said. "It's alright. You don't have to worry."

She looked up at me, her eyes bloodshot from cryin'. "They don't believe me, Mister Austin. They kept saying I did it, that I killed Samuelito! How could they say that?" She buried her face in my chest.

"Christ, almighty," Clay said. He and Brian exchanged a glance.

"Maria, which ones? Who said that?" I asked as the fury began to rise inside me.

She struggled for a breath. "Misters... Johnson and Colbert."

"Colbert?" Clay asked. "Are you sure there's a Colbert in that jury?"

She looked at him and nodded. "Second man, the one with the yellow hair and blue eyes. He was mean, and kept saying I did it, and that I should just admit it before an innocent man is..." she continued to cry.

"You know him?" Brian asked.

Clay shook his head. "I know of some Colberts. If he's from that same family, I can tell you without a doubt the jury's been compromised."

"Plan A?" Brian said again.

Clay looked around. Too many people had heard the conversation. "No. Not yet. Let this build. We already know what's going to happen."

The words, "The jury's been compromised" began being echoed across the crowd, causin' more and more calls for justice.

Thirty minutes later Anderson came out. "We're adjourned for the evening. We'll reconvene at nine in the morning."

The crowd got louder than ever, and I heard several shouts for justice, citin' that the jury had been bought, and that if they weren't gonna do the right thing, they would, and so forth. Just standard angry mob stuff. Anderson disappeared back inside. Probably for his own protection.

"Did Will come out?"Clay asked.

"No. He didn't," I said. "They probably snuck him out. What are we gonna do about them?" I looked at the crowd as they continued to yell.

"I say let them do what we were gonna," Brian said. "Plan B."

Clay chuckled for a moment. "Maybe that's the best idea. We can just go have some whiskey and watch from the boardwalk at Pearson's."

"It would make for some fine entertainment, that's for sure," I said.

A few moments later the Saloon doors opened, with Harold the bartender standin' there. "They all left, and we're open for business as usual if you all want a drink."

"Or we could stay here," Clay said.

"Sounds good to me," Brian said.

"Whiskey's whiskey," I said.

Several in the crowd cheered the good news and followed us in, apparently forgettin' about the lynchin' business at hand.

I looked down at Missus Kennedy, who was still clingin' to me. She'd heard it all too. "Ma'am, you should join us. I don't think it's a good idea for you to be alone this evenin'."

She nodded. "Thank you, Mister Austin." She looked at Clay. "And you, Mister Allison. I will repay you for your generosity."

He smiled his most charmin' smile and said, "Ma'am, I never said it was a loan. Consider it a gift, a recompense from the good spirits for the time you've had. For the terrible loss you've suffered."

She reached out for him, and he took her hand. "You are a good man, Clay Allison." She looked at all three of us. "You all are. God will shine his love down upon you."

"Come on," I said. "Let's get a table before there ain't none left."

Chapter 8

We four walked in and managed to find a table as the crowd poured in. The piano player immediately assumed his role and started playin' cheerful tunes. I heard the sound of billiard balls clackin' together from a back room, and saw a few couples dancin'. I always thought saloons should be more family type institutions. Just folks gathered to have a few drinks and generally enjoy themselves. I mean, other than the real youngins, if you know what I mean.

"Missus Kennedy, would you like a drink?" Clay asked.

She smiled at him. "Please. Just call me Maria. I don't want to hear his name again."

He nodded. "Maria."

"I would like some... beer." She grinned wide. "I never have beer."

"Beer it is. Boys? This round's on me."

"Tennessee Sour Mash," I said. "And since you're buyin', why not get a bottle?"

He chuckled. "Brian?"

"Who am I to pass up good ole Tennessee whiskey?"

Clay grinned. "Alright, then." He stood up and went to the bar.

Maria stared at him for a moment, and then me. "Since I got here I've heard stories about you two. Bad stories. Things you've done. People you've killed. But, I can see what you are now. You're God's avenging angels. You're like the archangel Michael." She grinned at me.

I smiled and said, "My mother actually named me after him. My middle name is Angelico."

"See? I knew it. You *are* angels. You do the dirty work, eliminating the evil from this world when nobody else will. The hand of God."

Brian chuckled. "High praise."

I had heard that term before, and it made me a little uneasy. Kennedy had said it. It was his excuse for killin' all them folks. Maybe it was some sort of biblical thing I'd overlooked in my younger days.

Maria looked at Brian. "I'm sorry, I don't know you."

He stood up and bowed, removin' his hat like a gentleman. "Forgive me. Brian Sanders." He put out his hand.

She grinned wide and shook his hand. "It's a pleasure to meet you, Mister Sanders."

"The pleasure is all mine Missus..." he hesitated. "I mean... Maria."

She nodded. "Cortez. My name was Cortez before..." she looked down. "Never mind."

"Let's just enjoy ourselves, why don't we?" I said. "I have a feelin' things will sort themselves out."

Clay came back with a nice, tall glass of beer for Maria, and a bottle of whiskey and three glasses. "Hey, who can resist the nectar of the gods?"

"Not I," I said.

"Nor I," Brian said.

Maria sipped on the beer and closed her eyes in pleasure. "I haven't had beer in so long. He would never let me have any. It was just his watered down whiskey, and he saved that for travelers or when he was in a foul mood. Of course, then he would only drink the good stuff he had hidden."

"Maria, may I ask you a personal question?" Brian asked.

She nodded.

"How old are you?"

"I just turned eighteen."

Us three men looked at each other. I was never so sad to have been right.

"So," I said. "How long have you been married to him?"

"Three years. Three terrible, horrible years."

"Let's talk about something else," Clay said.

"No. I want to tell you how my life was," she said. "All of it. Not just the little bit I told you before, but everything. You need to know the kind of demon that I was married to. You need to know why he has to die. You need to understand that whatever happens in that court, he *must die*." She put her hand on mine and looked up at me. "He *must die*. Send him back to Hell where he belongs."

"Oh, we'll make sure that happens," Clay said.

"You *must* kill Charles. You're the avenging angels sent by God to send him back to Hell. I know it to be true, you're his hand of justice. To do his will on Earth. God has answered my prayers," she said as she continued to look into my eyes. "Promise me, Michael Angelico. Promise me he will not leave this town alive. Promise me he will not ever lay a hand on another person or... kill another child." Tears streamed down her face. "Promise me you will kill him, not some angry mob that he might escape from. Promise me, and I will know it's true."

Tears began to roll down my cheeks too. I glanced up at the other two, who were nodding grimly. I took her hands in mine and said. "I... we promise you. We *will* kill him for you. We'll send him to Hell where he belongs."

She nodded, lowered her head, and wiped away her tears. "God has answered my prayers."

I reached into my vest pocket and pulled out the photograph I'd found. I handed it to her. She took it and looked up at me, her eyes wide. "Where did you find this?"

"I was lookin' for Jose and found it in his stuff. I figured he'd been killed, seein' as he's your..." I hesitated to say it out loud.

"He is my father." She looked up at me with questioning eyes. "But nobody here knows that."

I patted her hand. "And nobody will. Not from me, anyway."

Clay and Brian looked at each other, understandin' the importance. They nodded.

Maria's gaze went to the photograph. "Charles wanted this done. He wanted to prove to the world that I was his. His property. I'd never worn clothes like this before. I had to give them back after." She turned it over. "I had a friend in Taos who wrote this for me, and I gave it to mi Papi when Charles ordered me to." She struggled for a breath and crumpled the photograph in her hand. She abruptly stood up, walked over to the stove and opened it, and tossed the photograph in. She watched it burn for a moment before closin' the stove back up. She looked up at us and began her story. "I was bought by a man whose real name is Charles

Canady, not Kennedy, from my father just before I turned fifteen. I didn't know a word of English..."

She had been not exactly bought, but taken from her father as Charles had taken a likin' to her while she was workin' a saloon cleanin' up and such. He then paid for her as a sort of dowry. Make no mistake, though. This was just another form of slavery, and was all too common. How much he paid, she didn't say. I doubt she knew.

Jose was not fit to be a father to her, and figured this arrangement would be best for everyone. Apparently Charles was just charmin' enough and seemed well off enough, that Jose figured his girl would be taken care of.

Maria discovered all too soon how evil Charles Kennedy was. He treated her all nice and such at first, callin' her sweet names, givin' her compliments and such. But then on their weddin' night he brutally forced himself on her. Things went quickly downhill. He showed his evil side, forcin' himself on her whenever he had a notion to. Then the beatin's started. When he didn't get the dinner he wanted, he beat her. When he didn't get the marital prerogatives he wanted, he beat her. When she didn't get the chores done when he wanted, he beat her.

They lived in Taos for a spell, until Charles got the idea for the Traveler's Rest up in Palo Fletchado Pass. Then he demanded she go and help him build that cabin. She was his slave, but she took the abuse, haulin' rocks for the foundation, workin' the logs, and so forth. She thought, in her child-mind, that he was doin' all this 'cause he loved her and wanted to protect her. But that wasn't it at all. He saw her as nothin' more than slave labor and a place to park his manhood when he felt the urge. At one point he compared her to a farm animal.

She cooked and cleaned and did all he asked. The brutality continued, and then she saw it turned on others. When they began invitin' folks in to give them food and shelter, it was nice at first. Maria had company, even if it was temporary. But then one day Kennedy went on a rampage and killed a man for bein' 'too nice' to her. He went through his things, took his money and any valuables, and threw his body in the nearby creek to be devoured by animals.

Then when Charles and Maria came to town, he was less than nice to the shop keepers, and threatened at least one of them at gunpoint. When they got home, he beat her for bein' 'too pretty.'

It only got worse.

Soon she was tasked with doin' chores near the road when a traveler was spotted, and then invitin' him in. Inside, Charles would reprimand her, slap her, and demand she make food for the poor, weary guest and himself. When she did, she would be beat again for not doin' it right. But then he would find out what kind of riches the traveler had on him and if it was nothin' worth takin', he'd bid them farewell. Then, of course, he would take his liberties with her after beatin' her senseless.

When, in their sixth month of marriage he discovered she was with child, he forced her to drink an herb tea that would cause a miscarriage, and then beat her 'till she lost it. He didn't want another mouth to feed, and worse, he didn't want her dotin' on some 'worthless baby' instead of bein' his slave labor. Although he never came right out and called her that, it was pretty obvious to many folks who happened by. This forced miscarriage happened more than once, and Maria told us through heavy tears she had lost three children in this manner. The next time she discovered she was pregnant, she managed to convince him it was a good thing, a new source of income. A way for more chores to be done as the child grew.

By this time Kennedy's reputation had spread all through the area. Folks from Raton down to Santa Fe knew about Kennedy and his Spanish wife, and the way station he'd set up. His 'Traveler's Rest'. Most folks were loath to do anythin' about the way he treated Maria, 'cause abuse in this manner was nothin' unusual. It wasn't seen as abuse, just marital matters that didn't concern strangers. This is a sad statement, but this is how it was. Folks didn't know about his murderous side business, though. Had they known, this story would have turned out way different.

Samuel was born, to tears as Maria cried and worried about his fate. But, she was resolute. She would work harder to help Charles, now not just for self-preservation, but for the life of her child. But things didn't get better. As predicted, the time she took to care for Samuel was resented by Kennedy, and she suffered many more bruises. He regarded the child as a burden, and never once held him. On more than one occasion he called it a 'Half-breed abomination', or just simply, 'it'. '"It's cryin'. Shut it up." And so forth. She managed to get her chores done with Samuel in tow at all times, though.

Her life only got worse.

To her horror, Samuel wasn't immune to Kennedy's rages. His first beatin' was at seven months old. One night she managed to slip away with Samuel, but got only as far as the edge of the forest where Jose was waitin'. When Charles found out and called for her, she was terrified. Instead of leavin' with Jose, she went home. This time, though, he didn't beat her. He just said he'd gotten worried about them, and requested breakfast.

The times he was kind to her started happenin' more and more, and he began to regard Samuel as more of a child than a thing. One time he actually helped feed the child, and Maria saw a smile warm his face. Not a smile of greed or sexual satisfaction. It was somethin' else. Like a husband and father lurked somewhere under that evil skin. She held hope that he was changin', becomin' more like a decent man.

She was wrong.

Over the years her father Jose discovered just how sinister this man was. He not only watched in horror as Charles stole and cheated, but noticed that certain visitors never left. Many times he tried to get Maria to leave with him, but they were both terrified of what would happen if they did. So, time dragged on. Jose stayed close by takin' odd jobs now and again just so he could pay for enough food to stay near, to keep his daughter and grandson in sight.

On a snowy Christmas day in 1869, Jose found someone who would help him. Somehow Kennedy found out and killed the man before he ever got close. Desperate, and knowin' that there was now a child on the premises, Jose left the area to find someone who would help. Apparently he'd considered approachin' Clay and me several times, but was not sure it would turn out any better, considerin' our reputation. But as the warmer weather came and he saw how Clay was with women, he decided he'd trust us. Tom Pritchett came through town askin' for us, but we just missed him. Jose, realizin' that Tom knew us, somehow found the courage to talk to him.

Tom became one of Kennedy's last victims.

"And then he killed my Samuelito," Maria said through tears. "So, you see, he is not a man. He is a demon. He must be sent back to his master in Hell."

Clay gritted his teeth and scratched his head.

Brian slammed a glass of whiskey. "Did you tell all of this to the grand jury? "

She nodded.

I stared out at the street, where people were still yellin' and talkin' about justice. I sipped on my whiskey. "She's right. We have to do it. Us three. If we let this crowd go after him, he'll escape sure as I'm sittin' here."

The others looked outside.

"We have to stop this mob," Clay said.

We three stood up at the same time.

"We'll be right back," Clay said to Maria.

She nodded, eyes wide.

We walked outside and into the street as some self-appointed lynch chairman spoke up. "Charles Kennedy is guilty! He's murdered children, innocent travelers, and women! He's raped and pillaged, and has stolen from local businesses! We already know he's bought his freedom, are we going let that happen?"

"No!" the crowd yelled. They all started to move up the street.

Clay fired his gun in the air.

They all stopped.

"This ain't the way, boys. Stand down," Clay said.

"Ain't the way?!" the chairman yelled. "Weren't you the feller who brought him in? You saw what he done! If anyone knows this has to be done, you do!"

I pointed up the street where Deputy Houx stood at the jail with his rifle pointed at the crowd.

Clay looked too, and chuckled. He hadn't seen him. "I guarantee if anyone tries to lynch Kennedy, you'll end up in worse shape. Deputy Houx is a sharpshooter. One more step and you're dead."

"How many shots does he have in that gun?" the chairman asked.

"I don't see how that's pertinent," I said.

"He can't get all of us!"

Clay and I stepped aside.

"Alright. Who wants to die first, then?" Clay said, presentin' his hand at the deputy. "Who will be the sacrificial lamb so that the others can continue? Who shall it be? You, sir?" He pointed at someone at random.

The man stepped back, shakin' his head.

"Now, just wait a minute!" the chairman said. "That's an old trick. He wouldn't do it."

"Maybe not, but I sure as hell would," I said as I drew my gun and pointed it at the crowd. "Go on, try me."

Clay raised his gun at them too. "Go on."

"This ain't right!" the chairman said. "Why are you defending him? He deserves to die!"

"And once he's found guilty in a court of law, he will," Clay said.

"But, he's bought off the jury!" someone said.

They all agreed.

"Where's your proof?" I said.

"Well… we heard you two talking about it!"

"We were just talkin'."

The crowd seemed confused.

"Listen, folks," Clay said. "Our testimony is tomorrow. Let's just cool our heels until the grand jury reaches a decision. Can you at least give it a rest until then? Kennedy ain't going nowhere."

"But," the lynch chairman said. "If he ain't indicted, he'll continue his killing. We all know that. People have gone missing for years, people on their way to and from Taos. Now we know why, Clay. I don't understand why you ain't gone up there and lynched him already, and why you didn't take care of this when you went out to his place. God knows you've done worse. Come on, listen to reason."

"What I done or ain't has nothing to do with this," Clay said. "The fact is we need to let this proceed legally. Acting now will only make things worse. Now, go on. Get on home to your families and let us take care of this when the time comes. Understand?"

Lynch Chairman shook his head. "It ain't right.

They slowly started to disburse.

"Silver tongued devil," Brian said, who had never stepped off the boardwalk.

Lynch Chairman stepped up, his finger pointed at us. "We're goin', but we're only doing this 'cause we know and respect you fellers. But listen here. You know better'n anyone what he done. You know he can't be let free. If he ain't indicted, he'll be lynched. One way or t'other."

I put my hand on his shoulder and drew close. "Why don't you leave the lynchin' to the professionals?"

He shoved my hand off and walked off in a huff.

"I'm feelin' a mighty thirst, my friend," I said to Clay.

"Me too."

We walked in just in time to see a man talkin' to Maria in a raised voice, and she was cryin'. It was that no good Will Tolliver wearin' a Union cap. He stood up and glared at us.

"Step away from her, Mister Tolliver," I said.

"I can talk to whoever I want, Mister Austin. What right do you have telling me what to do?"

The three of us stepped forward.

"I'd advise you do what my associate asked ever so nicely," Clay said.

Another man stepped up next to Will and pulled on his shoulder.

He shrugged it off. "No, what right do they have? They're criminals! We're law abiding citizens!"

Clay walked right up and removed his hat, scratchin' his head. "Mister Tolliver, you're occupying the space where my seat is. Please remove yourself."

Tolliver stepped up and said, "Why don't you remove me, Mister Allison?"

Clay put his hat on the table as several folks decided now would be a good time to go home. He looked back at me and said, "For the record, I did ask nicely."

"Ah, hell," Brian said.

I reached out to Maria, and she stood up. I motioned to Brian. "Get her outta here."

Brian quickly escorted her toward the door just about the time Clay spun back around with his fist flyin' through the air.

There was a loud snap as Clay's fist impacted on Tolliver's jaw, followed by a moment of perfect silence. Not even the piano player was playin', as he had elected to evacuate the premises as well. But plenty other folks remained. As it turned out, most of the folks who were left behind were friends of Tolliver's.

Challenge: Accepted. I grinned as I realized this. I popped my knuckles and readied myself for a good old fashioned saloon fight. Sometimes there's nothin' better to get the kinks out.

Tolliver's head snapped around, and his body followed. He went down like a sack of taters, but he wasn't out. He jumped up and tackled Clay right into me, and the three of us slammed up against the bar. Stools went flyin'. Tolliver stumbled back, his lip now open and bleedin', and kicked Clay in the gut. This caused the two of us to stumble back again, prone and scramblin' to get our wits about us.

"Whoop him, Will! Show him who's boss!" someone yelled.

"Don't let these low lifes get the better of ya! Teach 'em a lesson they'll not soon forget!" another yelled.

He stood back and waited, his fists up. "Come on, boys. Let's see what you got." He bounced a few times like them prize fighters in San Francisco. He'd been trained in some sorta boxin'.

Clay snarled and scratched his head. "God damn Yankee scum son of a bitch."

"Here we go," I said.

"Sing us a fightin' song, Mike," Clay said.

"Iiiiiiii...."I started. "Wish I was in the land of cotton..."

Clay chuckled as we finally got to our feet. "Old times there are not forgotten."

"Look away, look away, look away, Dixie Land!" we both sang.

"Mine eyes have seen the glory of the coming of the lord!" Brian proudly sang as he walked in, hangin' his hat on the hook. He came and stood next to us, ready to fight alongside.

We glanced at each other and grinned.

"He is trampling out the vintage where the grapes of wrath are stored; He hath loosed the fateful lightning of His terrible swift sword: His truth is marching on!" Brain sang.

"In Dixie Land where I was born in, early on a frosty mornin', Look away, look away, look away, Dixie Land. Then I wish I was in Dixie, hooray! hooray! In Dixie Land I'll take my stand to live and die in Dixie, Away, away, away down South in Dixie, Away, away, away down South in Dixie!" Clay and I sang together.

Tolliver and the others stood and watched in incredulity. A couple others stepped up next to him, loosenin' their sleeves.

It started all at once.

The six of us practically jumped at each other, throwin' fists of fury. Clay landed a solid hit on Tolliver, who spun around and hit him solid. They were like two prize fighters, tradin' punch for punch.

The feller who had designs on teachin' me a lesson got in a good punch square in my nose, causin' me to stumble back. He then rapid punched me over and over again, 'till I fell on my ass.

Brian ran at his feller and ducked just as he punched, and then punched upward, sendin' his feller onto our table. It held his weight, but that high dollar whiskey Clay had bought suffered a different fate. It shattered on the floor.

That pissed me off. I gritted my teeth and jumped up, right into my feller's fists. I fell on my ass again, shakin' my head to try and figure out what I was doin' wrong.

The doors flung open again, and several from the angry mob rushed in, ready for a fight. In times like these when emotions are high, you gotta expect this sort of thing.

I shook my head as I heard a chorus of men screamin' a war cry, followed by a series of crashes. I'm pretty sure someone actually yelled, 'yahoooo!' I managed to get to my feet with my fists in front of me. It was chaos. The entire saloon was gettin' involved. My feller was still focused on me, though. I put up my hand in defense and motioned to a bar stool. Confused, he stepped forward. I grabbed a random bottle of whiskey and poured ourselves two glasses. I handed him one. "Seems only fair," I said. "You kicked my ass."

He grinned and took the drink. We tapped them together and drank down, resolved to watch the festivities unfoldin' before us.

As the saloon patrons became engaged in mortal battle, complete with bottles and chairs flyin', I put out my hand. "Mike Austin."

He smiled and shook it. A nice, strong grip with rough hands. A workin' man. "Justin Fellows." He had a subdued Alabama drawl.

"Pleasure to get my ass kicked by you, sir."

He laughed. "Pleasure's all mine." He motioned to the fight. "North and South fightin' side by side. Never thought I'd see it."

"Said the Alabamy boy," I said.

"Montgomery, and you? I'm thinkin' Georgia?"

I raised my glass. "Augusta born and raised."

"Old times there are not forgotten, good sir." He raised his glass.

I raised mine too. "Fellows. I seem to remember a Fellows durin' the Hill Campaign."

His eyes got wide. "You're shittin' me. *Sergeant* Austin?"

I nodded. "The very same."

He grinned wide. "Corporal Fellows. I was right next to you when they took us to prison, right after Lieutenant Daniels' was damn near killed."

"I'll be damned. So, you were in Andersonville."

"Yes, sir." He shook his head. "You mean Hell."

"That it was, Corporal. That it most surely was."

"So, whatever happened to Daniels? I lost track of him after he recovered."

"He finally got promoted up to Captain just before it all ended. He's got a ranch now in Agua Dulce. A wife, kids, the whole nine yards."

"Next time you see 'im, say hello for me, if you would."

"Not sure if or when I will, to be honest, but I'll give him your regards. Say, what the hell are you doin' with Tolliver?"

He shrugged. "He paid us to be his bodyguards, against folks like you who'd want to do 'im in for speakin' up in support of Kennedy. Me and a bunch of other drifters are on his payroll. It's just a job. Said he was tryin' to get Kennedy off so he could take care of 'im his own way. I guess Kennedy owes him money."

I laughed. "Now it makes sense. Well, I won't say nothin' about it, then."

After several more minutes of saloon fightin' chaos, my new friend and I were laughin' pretty hard at the shenanigans. Clay and Tolliver were still in the clutches of doom, but I knew it would either end with the two of them sharin' a drink, or someone dead. No sense spoilin' the end.

Suddenly there was a big BOOM from a shotgun. It had come from the door. Everyone ducked and looked.

Deputy Houx stood there reloadin'. "What the hell is wrong with you people? Stop this shit right now or so help me, I'll stop it for you!" He snapped the shotgun back into place.

"Awe, come on, Deputy," I said. "We were just blowin' off some steam. Come have a drink with us."

"Mike Austin, I would expect better of you. And Clay... just... get yourselves together and clean this shit up."

"Hey, at least he didn't ride his horse in here like last time," I said in a chuckle. "Naked except for his gun belt."

Clay stood up, his eye already swellin' and his lip bleedin'. He and Tolliver were probably the only ones not just blowin' off steam. He glared at his opponent. "How about you and I finish this outside, Tolliver?"

Tolliver spat blood. "Gladly."

"Hold on there," the deputy said. "The last thing this town needs is a shooting in the street. Mister Tolliver, you and your boys skedaddle. Clay and the rest of you, just stay put for now."

Clay pointed at Tolliver. "I better not see you again."

Tolliver spat on the floor. "Come on, boys."

Justin slammed one last drink and grinned at me before he left. "Sergeant."

I chuckled. "Corporal."

After a few moments, hearin' the horses trot off, Deputy Houx lowered his shotgun. "I got enough damn trouble keeping Charles Kennedy alive while the whole territory wants him dead, and it ain't because I want him alive! It's because it's my job! I don't need this shit! You boys stay behind and clean this place up, and then get on home or... wherever. And don't give me no more trouble, or so help me God!"

We did like he said. Hey, it helped blow off some steam. We all knew tomorrow was comin', and everythin' would change. Someone would die.

Chapter 9

After a severe reprimand from Carmen and a pointed question as to where her dishes were, she cleaned me up good.

"I'm getting tired of being your nursemaid, Mike Austin," she said as she dabbed my cuts with a damp cloth. "Got your ass handed to you this time, huh?"

"Yep. I'll admit it. That feller knew just how hard to punch me." I smiled.

"And where. Looks like your nose is damn near broke. What is it with you boys and your fights? Especially at a time like this?"

"For most of us it was just about blowin' off steam. For Clay and Will Tolliver, it was clearly somethin' more. I mean, Will actually defended Charles Kennedy."

"They do have a pretty good defense, other than Jose's testimony. They attacked his

150

character pretty bad, tripped him up. It ain't going to count."

"How would you know that?"

"Jamie Stephens is on the jury, one of our... clients. He's worried this'll go south and Kennedy will get off."

"Yeah, I reckon we all are. Ouch!" I said as she dabbed some alcohol on my forehead.

"Hurts, don't it, big boy?"

"Carmen, I think this might have to be resolved another way."

"You mean like a lynching?"

I didn't respond.

"There's a whole town of folks, men and women, ready to do that."

"Missus Kennedy asked Clay and Brian and me to do it ourselves. To not let a mob do it, on accounta Charley might escape."

She stopped cleanin' me and looked in my eyes. "Are you serious?"

I nodded. "She made us promise. Called us avenging angels."

"So, you're going to do it, then. Really going to do it." Her eyes were wide.

"The boys and my testimony are tomorrow mornin'. We made a plan to take care of things if'n it all goes wrong like we suspect. But nobody can know, understand?"

She nodded. "So, she actually asked you to do it. Wow."

"I've been conflicted about this whole thing from the beginnin', Carmen. Clay and I both. Davy had the clearest mind about it from the get go. We shoulda strung up Kennedy when we first found him. I know that now."

"But then you'd be in jail right now, for murder." She caressed my face. "It wouldn't have been right."

"Nah, once the bodies had been found and everyone heard what Missus Kennedy had to say, it would have been dismissed. This ain't my first rodeo."

She giggled.

"But a lynchin' now, before the grand jury finishes, would be complicated. If the whole town banded together and done it, nothin' further would happen. That's the best idea. But in the chaos it's a good possibility Kennedy would slip away. That's what we're worried about. Then what? A manhunt across these mountains in winter? He'd be gone. Kennedy knows how to survive in these conditions, and worse, he's likely to find a way to get to the missus."

"But if the two of you —"

"Three. Brian Sanders is helpin'."

"He is?" She shook her head. "Poor man. Kennedy killed his son."

"Yep. But if just us three do it, we'll be in some trouble. Murder charges, like you said. If the jury returns without an indictment, and we can somehow shine a light on the fact that there's corruption, maybe this lynchin' will be… justified."

"Folks will look the other way."

"Either way, Carmen. It's gonna happen tomorrow."

"God in Heaven," she said.

"And it ain't gonna be pretty."

I didn't sleep much that night. And it weren't just 'cause of Carmen's lovin'. I knew what was comin', and couldn't stop thinkin' about how it would.

By nine in the mornin' I was shined up, shaved, bathed, and wearin' my best duds. Carmen had some nice uncomfortable shiny shoes for me to wear too. She even trimmed my hair and everythin'. Other than my obvious bruises and cuts from the night before, I looked damn fine. I even left my hat and gun belt at the massage parlour. I felt like I was about ready to go to church and get my soul saved. Maybe I shoulda. Carmen stood near me, her arm around mine.

Clay and Brian were there too, and I reckon they'd gotten the same idea. We were three proper lookin' country gentlemen dandies ready to testify the God's honest truth before a grand jury.

I would not be exaggeratin' to say the entire town was there too, fillin' the street outside Middaugh Saloon. There was no talk of lynchin' this mornin', though. All talk was about how the grand jury would rule after the three of us said our peace.

I looked up at the overcast sky, wonderin' if it would come a full blizzard before it was all said and done.

"March, can you believe it?" someone said. "I heard that if they do indict, he wouldn't stand trial until March. Are we going to feed that fat bastard for half a year? And what if he escapes? Where's that other deputy? I thought we had another one in this town."

"No, Anderson said he was going to move to have the trial now," someone said.

"But then, what if he isn't indicted, and what about bail?" another person asked.

"There's no damn way they'd grant him bail."

"So, then we'd have to give him a room 'till spring. Who's gonna pay for that?"

"No, Anderson said. They'd have trial now."

And so on.

It was all talk like this, and how our testimony would influence the proceedin's. Would our words be enough to sway the jury? And it was also about reputation. Kennedy's reputation, like ours, was well known these days. There wasn't one person in northern New Mexico Territory who hadn't heard of us all now. The newspaper was the biggest culprit, printin' all kinds of sensational stories about how Maria had climbed out through the chimney to escape, or had crawled thirty miles through six foot high snow durin' a blizzard only to be turned away by three other establishments before arrivin' at Pearson's, or how she was actually a Ute woman and had run away from her tribe.

There were stories about how a missin' senator had been buried under Kennedy's garden, and how the President himself had colluded to free Kennedy. The words 'Presidential Pardon' was heard on several occasions.

Clay, Brian and me just sighed and tried to ignore it all, but it was damn difficult when strangers started askin' us questions. But we did. We simply remained quiet.

"I'm surprised we ain't heard anything about the Maxwell Grant situation," Clay said.

"Oh, hell no," Brian said. "This is front page news these days."

Anderson stepped out. "We're in session again. Brian Sanders, you're up."

And so it began.

Brian cleared his throat, checked his hair with the palm of his hand, and glanced at us. "Here we go." He disappeared inside.

Although I wasn't inside to see and hear what happened, Brian told me later. Here's how it went:

ANDERSON: Grand jury is now in session, the date is October seven, the year of our Lord eighteen hundred seventy.

(Anderson walked up to Brian with a bible in his hand)

ANDERSON: Please place your left hand on the bible and raise your right hand.

(Brian did)

ANDERSON: Please state your full name for the record.

BRIAN: Brian Wilbur Sanders.

ANDERSON: Mister Sanders, in the testimony you are about to give, do you swear to tell the truth, the whole truth, and nothing but the truth so help you God?

BRIAN: I do so swear.

ANDERSON: Please be seated.

(He did. He was in a regular chair facin' the jury, who sat on bar stools behind the bar. They then began to ask questions. Anderson went and sat at a table, next to Mills. They remained quiet)

JOHNSON: Mister Sanders, how do you know the defendant, Charles Kennedy?

BRIAN: He killed my son.

JOHNSON: Did you see Mister Kennedy commit this act?

BRIAN: No, sir. But he disappeared on his way from Eagle Nest to Taos earlier this year. When I went looking for him, I came upon Mister Kennedy's home-

JOHNSON: So, your son disappeared, and you automatically assumed Kennedy had something to do with it?

BRIAN: No, not exactly. See, when I got there, I saw his Momma's pendant in the dirt near Kennedy's front porch. It was covered in blood.

JOHNSON: So, you're testifying that you did not see Mister Kennedy kill your son or otherwise have anything to do with his disappearance.

BRIAN: That's not what I said. See, then I knocked on his door, and Missus Kennedy opened it. He yelled at her and she closed it, but I saw a small boy inside crying.

JOHNSON: Thank you, Mister Sanders. Do any other jury members wish to question this witness?

STEPHENS: Yes, I do. Mister Sanders, I'd like to hear more about your story.

JOHNSON: That's not a question.

STEPHENS: I'd still like to hear it.

BRIAN: So, I knocked again and Kennedy answered the door. He had blood splattered on him, and was quite rude. He pointed a gun at me and demanded I leave his property. So, I did. But after hearing what I did about him and what he was... accused of, I knew what had happened. He killed my son and took his money.

COLBERT: This is all just conjecture, Mister Sanders. Just because he's accused of something doesn't mean he's guilty. Thank you, you're excused.

(Brian sat there, flabbergasted)

ANDERSON: Mister Sanders, you're excused.

(Brian stood up, shook his head, and walked toward the door. Anderson followed)

The door opened and Brian emerged, a deep scowl on his face. He looked at Clay and me and shook his head.

"Mister Austin," Anderson said.

I walked up.

He nodded and opened the door for me, I walked in. We walked just in front of the bar, where a chair sat facin' it. Behind the bar was the grand jury, twenty one folks who looked more out of place than I did. The saloon itself was still in a state of disarray from the previous day's festivities, and I chuckled to myself.

"Please place your left hand on this bible, and raise your right hand," Anderson said.

I did.

"Please state your full name for the record."

"Michael Angelico Thurman Austin."

"Mister Austin. In the testimony you are about to give, do you swear to tell the truth, the whole truth, and nothing but the truth so help you God?"

"Yes, sir. I do so swear."

"Please be seated."

I did.

Anderson went and sat with Mills. They looked more like best buddies than adversaries.

"Mister Austin," Colbert said. "We have read your statement given to Deputy Houx. We just have but one question for you, sir. Did you personally see Mister Kennedy commit any act of murder?"

I instantly felt the rage boil inside me. "Well, no, but we found bodies of—"

"So, that's a no, then?"

I gritted my teeth and tried to maintain my composure. "No."

"Thank you. You're excused."

"He paid you off, didn't he?" I snarled.

They looked at each other, all but Stephens who kept his gaze on me.

"Mister Austin, you are out of order," Johnson said. "You've been dismissed. Please leave this court."

Anderson stood up and started walkin' toward me. "Mister Austin, you've been excused." He motioned to the door.

"Wait a minute, god damn it! You're nothin' but a bought jury! This whole thing is bullshit! You know damn well he done it!"

"Mister Austin!" Anderson insisted.

I nodded and exited, glarin' at Clay. I shook my head. I didn't see Brian anywhere. Carmen stood with her eyes wide. The crowd began to get loud with conversation, several yellin', askin' why my testimony only took a short time.

"Mister Allison," Anderson said.

Clay walked up and put his hand on my shoulder. He glanced at the slaughterhouse.

I nodded.

Clay told me later how it went inside. It weren't much different than mine. They just asked him if he'd actually seen Kennedy kill anyone. He answered honestly, and they dismissed him.

Before I'd gotten to Carmen, I already heard Clay inside yellin' and carryin' on about how the grand jury had been bought. I finally got to her and took her hand.

"What the hell happened?" she asked.

"It's just like we thought. At least a couple of them are on Kennedy's payroll."

"Dear God!" Carmen said in a gasp. "Are you sure?"

"They only asked one question, if we'd seen him kill anyone. They didn't ask about his house, the bodies, or anythin' else."

"Shit."

"Carmen, go home. Things are about to get ugly."

"Mike, please be careful." She gave me a kiss and ran off.

The crowd was gettin' rowdy, startin' to talk about a lynchin' again. I sneaked off toward the slaughterhouse.

Chapter 10

I heard Clay yell a few more times as he exited, and then Anderson said the jury would retire for deliberation. The crowd continued to get louder. I continued on toward the slaughterhouse. There was a sudden dip in temperature. A chill in the air. The chill of death.

I walked in and found it empty except for Brian, who had already fashioned a noose, hangin' it over one of the high slaughterin' beams. The other end of the rope was run through a pulley at ground level.

"Let me guess, just one question," Brian said.

I nodded. "Yep. If I'd actually seen him kill anyone."

"I figured. I guess we wait for Clay now."

His sentence wasn't finished when Clay walked in, his face red with anger. "They've been bought," he said. "This is happening."

"We need to wait for the announcement that he ain't been indicted," I said. "Don't we?"

He nodded. "But we'll have to be quick about it. If it comes back no, and we already know it will, we'll need to get Kennedy out of there before that mob rushes the jail and more folks get killed at the deputy's hand."

"Jesus, this could turn into a slaughter," Brian said.

"I reckon we're in the right place, then," I said.

"Maybe we should go get him now, just in case," Brian said.

We all looked at each other.

"I agree," Clay said. "Let's go get him now, while everyone's distracted waiting for official word."

"I'll go in first," I said. "You boys get ready to sneak him around the back, away from the eyes of the crowd."

"He's a big feller, Mike. Can you handle him alone?" Clay asked.

"I just have to get him to the door. You boys can help me with the rest."

"How you going to handle the deputy?" Brian asked.

"I'll just explain the facts. Let him decide," I said.

"And you think he'll agree?"

"If we rush the jail, he'll defend it. But if I just mosey in and tell him what's needin' to happen, I think he'll make the right decision."

"So, what about Justice McBride? Ain't he over there too?"

"I doubt it, but if he is, same deal."

"Wait. I hear something," Clay said.

There was a rise in the angry voices comin' from the saloon. We looked out and saw Anderson evidently explainin' the situation.

"No decision yet," Clay said. "We have to move now before that crowd does."

"Kennedy'll be yelling, calling for help," Brian said. He looked around the buildin'. "You'll need to gag him."

Clay produced his handkerchief. "This'll do."

I grabbed it. "Let's go." I walked out first, casual as you please, just out for a stroll. I made my way across the street, seein' the crowd gettin' louder and louder as Anderson tried to calm them down. I opened the door and moseyed on into the jail house.

Kennedy sat on his bed. Apparently someone had brought him a fluffy mattress. He was all reclined and smug, smilin' at me. "So, can I go home now?" There was a tall stack of dishes near the door.

Only Deputy Houx was there guardin' him. "What's happening out there, Mike?"

"The grand jury is deliberatin'," I said. "But it's a near sure thing he'll not be indicted."

Houx nodded. "You and Clay already testified, then?"

I nodded.

He sighed. "Then, it's time, ain't it?"

I nodded. "I came to spell you, Deputy." My hand went down to where my gun usually was, but of course I didn't have it for testimony.

He noticed I wasn't armed. "I could use a trip to the outhouse." He glanced at the rifles and revolvers in the rack. "A long trip to the outhouse." He sat the key to the cell on the table and stood up. He and I stared at each other for a moment, and then he nodded. He opened the door and glanced at Kennedy, and then back at me. "Better hurry. You don't have much time."

I nodded as he left.

"See, I told you I'd be walking out a free man," Kennedy said. "It's just a matter of time before they return with no indictment. Then I'll sue you and your pals, Mike Austin. You'll be the ones in jail. How does that sound, huh? Then I can finally be reunited with my lovely wife. Won't she be surprised? That damned whore."

I walked over to the gun rack and picked a nice, new Henry rifle. I grabbed some ammo and quickly filled the magazine, feedin' rounds in one right after the other. Then I scooped up the chains and tossed them into the cell. "Put 'em on, Kennedy. I have to escort you."

"But, I'll be a free man, why would you have to escort me?"

"Thems the rules." I pointed the rifle at him. "Put 'em on."

He reluctantly put the shackles on, loosely. "You'll pay for this, Austin. You'll see."

"Put your hands through the bars," I ordered.

I could hear the crowd gettin' louder, and couple of gunshots were fired in anger. They were already movin' up the street.

He chuckled. "See? They're already celebrating. Justice is served today, Austin." He put his hands through the bars so I could secure his wrist shackles. "You'll be taking these off directly."

"Back away," I ordered.

A smug smile on his face, he nodded and backed away. I unlocked the cell and backed up. I motioned with the rifle. "Come on, don't make me shoot you."

"Maybe I should, so you can feel the noose for murder."

"Come on out, turn around."

He frowned. "Turn around? What? Why?"

"I said do it!"

He reluctantly turned around, and I quickly, forcefully, wrapped the gag around his mouth. Fearin' the worst, he slammed backwards, knockin' me against the wall. I dropped the rifle. He then spun around and hit me hard on the side of the head with the shackles. I fell back again.

"Help! Help!" he yelled as he ran for the door. "He's going to kill me! Help!"

I managed to get the rifle in my hands, but had no time to turn, aim, and shoot. So I just threw it at him like a dumbass. It hit his leg and he stumbled. But he didn't go down. Instead he grabbed the rifle as best he could and pointed it at me.

"I see what's happening now. You're trying to lynch me before the decision comes back ain't you?"

"Face what you did, Charley," I said. "Face it like a man. You killed your own child, for God's sake!" I scrambled to get to my feet.

"No, you just stay right there, Austin. That thing wasn't my child. It was a half-breed abomination. They don't have no souls, didn't you know that?"

My anger boiled.

"I think it's time you face what you done. What you really are. No more games." He rotated back the hammer and pulled the trigger.

It went click.

It was loaded, but no rounds were in the chamber. I quickly got to my feet and rushed him, but he was ready for me. He met me with a solid hit with the rifle stock, knockin' me to the side. He struggled to rotate the lever, to chamber a round.

The crowd was approachin', their voices of protest and blood lust growin' louder by the second.

I spun my leg around, catchin' him. He tripped, pullin' the trigger. The loud report of the gunshot would surely be heard. But at least it went up into the ceilin' and not into me.

We commenced to wrestlin' like two drunk bastards in a saloon fight. But this wasn't about blowin' off steam. This was a fight to the death. I finally got on top of him and began hittin' him in the face as hard as I could. But then he somehow managed to get his leg up and knocked me right off, into the desk. The lamp fell off and shattered on my head, and everythin' started gettin' blurry as blood and coal oil poured down my face.

I heard him strugglin' with the shackles to get the key, to get them off. I had to act fast, despite my growin' head pain. I managed to stand up and rush him, but he was too fast. He simply stepped aside, yankin' one of the revolvers from the rack. He held it with a sloppy grip, but it would be good enough to end me.

"Now I got you, Austin. You abomination, god damn bastard. Go back to where you came from." He rotated back the hammer and pulled the trigger.

I flinched at the last second, and the bullet went through my side, just under my arm pit. My pain multiplied, and I yelled from it. I staggered through the pain and all, but managed to slam into him, causin' him to fall back. The room was full of smoke, now, complicatin' the fight further. The floor was soaked in blood. As I struggled to get up, he managed to get his arms around my neck. He started squeezin'.

"Die, demon!" he screamed.

I felt the life startin' to leave me, but I had one more trick. I managed to push my legs up with all my remainin' energy, straight up. I flipped over him, and fell into the gun rack. It crashed to the floor. I searched for a gun, but everythin' was gettin' increasingly blurry. I shook my head as I heard a gun hammer click back.

"Bastard," Kennedy said.

The door flung open with Clay rushin' in. Kennedy spun around and pointed the gun at him, but Clay was a professional, you see. In a blur of motion he simply reached up, yanked the gun out of Kennedy's hands, and pistol whipped him. Kennedy went out, collapsin' on the floor next to me.

"Jesus, boy, what the hell's going on here? I thought you said you could handle him!" Clay said.

I gritted my blood soaked teeth and slipped on the slick floor, tryin' to get to my feet. "I was handlin' him!"

"I can see that. Damn nasty gash on the head, all shot up to hell and all. I don't think this is how to do it, Mike. Come on, we have no more time, we gotta get his ass outta here now!" He put out his hand and helped me up. He looked at my head and side. "Damn, Sergeant. What the hell were you thinkin'?" He shoved his spare handkerchief at me. "Stuff up that hole, soldier."

I grabbed it and stuffed it under my shirt, over the hole. It was only a graze, thankfully, but it still hurt like hell and caused me to bleed like a stuck pig.

Clay grabbed Kennedy's arm. "Come on, grab a hunk!"

I could see the crowd outside, and there would be no sneakin' Kennedy out now. Clay and I took an arm and started draggin' him across the road. Brian saw me strugglin' and ran to spell me. I backed away and let him, glancin' at the outhouse where Deputy Houx was. I could see the top of his head as he spied through the little crescent moon air hole in the top. He wouldn't emerge 'till it was all done.

"String him up! String him up!" the crowd chanted as they marched toward us. But then as they saw us haulin' him across the road, they broke into a run.

I reached down to my... damn. I still wasn't armed. Damned inconvenient. Instead, I ran to hold the door open for Clay and Brian as they drug Kennedy inside. I bolted it shut behind them, gaspin' for a breath. "Christ!" I said.

"Come on, let's do this now," Clay said.

We drug him over to the noose, and wrapped it around his neck, tightenin' it good. It took all three of us to hoist that big son of a bitch up with the noose, but about halfway, he woke up and started flailin', clawin' at the rope with his shackled hands.

"Let me go!" he screamed the best he could as the rope began stranglin' him. "God will get his vengeance! Shay Lamb is coming!"

"That shit again," I said. "This bastard's a lunatic."

"What the hell is shaylam?" Brian asked.

"Hell if I know. Let's just get this done," I said.

"Pull!" Clay yelled.

We bore down, heavin' the rope through that squeekin', protestin' pulley as Kennedy yelled and struggled. His feet finally lifted off. He started swingin' them, tryin' to find traction like he was treadin' water. At least the noose finally tightened enough that he stopped yellin'. We made sure, pullin' 'till his feet were a good five feet above the floor. I tied it off, and we backed away, winded. Kennedy's face began to turn blue, and his eyes bugged out. Still, he struggled to catch a breath.

"Damn he's a big boy, ain't he?" Clay said.

"That he is," Brian said. He looked at me. "And he sure beat the hell outta you."

"You noticed." I grimaced in pain.

The crowd started bangin' on the door, demandin' entry. We all looked at each other.

I shrugged. "He ain't gettin' away now."

"Open the door," Clay said.

Brian nodded and did so.

The mob rushed in, ready to do who knew what. But as soon as the first ones entered, they went quiet. They watched as Charles Kennedy struggled to continue livin', kickin' his feet and thrashin' about.

"Jesus, Mary and Joseph," one said as he did the sign of the cross. "You did it, you actually did it."

"I can't... watch this," One said. He promptly vomited in horror.

Slowly they filed in, witnessin' the final moments of the killer known as Charles Kennedy. He struggled, still fightin' and gaspin' for air. After a few more agonizin' minutes, his body suddenly went limp, his shackled hands fallin' to his belly. He was dead. His face was purple and his eyes looked like they were about to pop out of his skull. Urine and feces dripped down from his pant legs, makin' a little puddle below him.

"It woulda been better to drop him from the second floor, snapping his neck," Brian said. "This way he was essentially just strangled."

"Hell no," Clay said. "This way was better. He suffered."

"God damn right," I said.

"And how do you think we woulda got him up there?" Clay asked.

"Fair point." Brian spat Kennedy's direction. "That's what you get, you piece of shit."

After a few minutes of people cyclin' through to see the spectacle, Deputy Houx walked in with Anderson and Mills directly behind.

"Christ almighty," Houx said. He looked at us, unbelievin'.

"The grand jury voted for indictment, despite some conflict between jurors," Anderson said. "He would have gone to trial." He shook his head and glared at each of us three. "This was senseless." He turned around and left.

"You three will be charged with murder!" Mills said.

"What murder?" Houx said.

"Are you blind? They hung him! This was a lynch mob, and you let it happen!"

"Clearly there was a struggle in the jailhouse," Houx said. "He escaped and hung himself. It was suicide, as he was wrought with guilt for what he done."

Mills looked under Kennedy, seein' no stool or anythin' that he could have used to climb up. Just a puddle of Kennedy's final evacuation. "This was murder!" He spun around and rushed out.

Deputy Houx looked at me as the blood flowed down my face and side. "You should get that looked at." He looked up at Kennedy's body. "Get him down, boys. The deed is done."

Clay found a large butcher knife and sliced through the rope. Kennedy's body collapsed. He looked at the knife and said, "I'll be right back."

173

He rushed out as fast as he could, his limp more pronounced than usual.

Outside, the snow started fallin' again, but lightly. The roads had already just begun to thaw again, but now it was turnin' colder.

"Where'd Clay go?" Brian asked.

"I don't know." I readjusted the handkerchief, that was now completely soaked. I wiped the lingerin' coal oil mixed with blood outta my face with my free hand. I was feelin' mighty poorly, but I held on to see what Clay was plannin'.

"What do we do with him?" Brian asked. He kicked the body.

"Bury him near the cemetery," Houx said. "When the ground thaws enough." He looked outside. "That could be a while yet."

Tim Burleson walked in. "Christ in Heaven." His face was pale. "What have you boys done?"

We heard hoof steps, and Clay came back in. "Everyone needs to know what happened here," he said as he looked at me. "Right?"

I nodded. "Right. Everyone."

"What are you going to do, Clay?" Houx asked.

"What I should have done a week ago." He reached over and grabbed the rope, the noose still around Kennedy's neck. "Help me, boys. He's going on one last journey. Let's make this perfectly clear what happens to baby killers around here."

"Oh, Jesus. Clay, you can't do that," Houx said.

"Then stop me, Deputy." He glared at him.

Houx just shook his head.

We drug Kennedy's body outside, where we had an audience of at least half the town. Clay tied the rope to his horse's saddle horn.

"Charles Kennedy will never hurt another soul," I said.

Clay mounted his horse. "This is what happens to baby murderers around here. Heeeeyah!" He kicked his horse, and he took off at a full run, Kennedy's body flailin' behind.

"Oh, my god," someone said. "This isn't happening."

"We thought this was what you wanted," Brian said. "He killed my son, he killed his own son. A baby. He beat his wife nearly to death. What was the mob about if not this?"

Clay Allison drug Kennedy's body through town, down every road, lappin' over and over again, 'til the body was an unrecognizable hunk of meat barely hangin' on the noose. Brian and I walked over to Lambert's Inn to let Maria know what had happened, but we saw her watchin' from her window, a somber look on her face.

There was not one adult in Elizabethtown who did not see.

Clay stopped his parade of blood in front of us, and dismounted. He looked at Brian. "We need a sign." He pulled the butcher knife out from his belt loop and looked at me. "Everyone needs to know."

I nodded. "Do it."

We walked back to the macabre remains of the killer Charles Kennedy. His head was holdin' on just by the few strands of flesh on his neck, and his spine. I grabbed what was left of his head and twisted it hard, snappin' the bone while Clay used the knife and did the rest.

Kennedy was beheaded.

Another crowd of people with yet unquenched morbid curiosity gathered around.

Brian found a small slab of wood, and Clay handed him the bloody knife. He carved, 'This is what happens to baby killers 'round here.' He used the blade to extract a nail from the entry fence to Lambert's Inn, and then used it to nail the sign on.

Clay took Kennedy's head and held it high for all to see. "Justice is served. Charles Kennedy is dead!"

There were no cheers, no exclamations of approval. There was nothin' but facial expressions of horror and disgust. Nobody made a sound.

Clay then took the head and impaled it on the entry fence. Blood trickled down the wood and over the new sign as Kennedy's now empty eye sockets stared out into oblivion.

We looked up at Maria's window.

She nodded.

Chapter 11

My wounds were more severe than what Carmen could deal with. I sat in Doctor Westerling's office as he stitched up the nasty cut on my head, havin' already dealt with my gunshot wound.

"Looks like Kennedy gave you something to remember him by," he said as he pulled the stitch across my skull.

"God damn that hurts!" I exclaimed.

"Drink some more whiskey."

"I'd have to be passed out for this shit not to hurt, Doc."

"I imagine that's true. That glass went all the way to the bone. He nearly scalped you."

"I had him right where I wanted him," I said as I took another swig from the bottle.

"Don't move so much."

"You just told me to drink more!"

He said some frustrated words in Norwegian or somethin'.

177

"Yeah, yeah. I know." I tried to remain as still as I could, meanwhile drinkin' an entire bottle of Jameson Whiskey. "Ain't you got any Sour Mash?"

"This isn't a saloon, Mister Austin."

Truth be told, I was gettin' pretty drunk off the stuff. "I just wish I'd killed that son of a bitch when I first met him. Then that boy'd still be alive."

"You and many, many other people feel the same way."

I sighed. "If I'd only known."

"Has Mister Allison gone home?"

"Yeah. He lit out just after plantin' Charley's head on a pole. Brian too."

"You're going too?"

"I have to get to El Paso, as soon as the weather lets up. Then I'll be back. Seems we got a war brewin' over land disputes."

"It's always something, Mister Austin."

"Ain't it though?"

He finished up and placed a bandage around my head. "This will need to be changed often, and you need to keep it clean. And don't worry, your hair will grow back."

I chuckled and grabbed my hat as I stood up, plantin' it on my head. It didn't fit right with the bandage, and sat sideways. "No problem, Doc. How much do I owe you?"

"This one is on me, Mister Austin. For what you did for this town. Everyone's going back to their lives, but nobody will ever forget what happened here." He pointed at the hat. "That hat has to go. Look at it. It's filthy. How long have you had it?"

I chuckled. "I can't remember."

"Get a new one, and get some rest."

"Rest sounds like a damn good idea. Thanks, Doc."

He nodded and I walked out into the snow storm. The roads weren't busy, just a few people walkin' here and there. But there was the bright red streak of Kennedy's blood and various pieces of flesh goin' right down the middle. It wouldn't go away 'til the road thawed. A few stray dogs licked at it and gobbled up the raw meat. One happily chomped on an eyeball. Hey, they gotta eat, don't they?

I walked over to Carmen's and practically fell into her arms. She took good care of me, after chastisin' me about her dishes.

It was a couple more weeks before there came an Indian summer of sorts. The ground was soft enough to bury Kennedy, my friend Tom Pritchett, and Samuel.

Chapter 12

We stood at the grave of Samuel Canady, his real name. The entire population of E-Town was in attendance as Pastor Ferlon prayed, "The Lord is my shepherd; I shall not want. He maketh me to lie down in green pastures: he leadeth me beside the still waters. He restoreth my soul: he leadeth me in the paths of righteousness for his name's sake. Yea, though I walk through the valley of the shadow of death, I will fear no evil: for thou art with me; thy rod and thy staff they comfort me. Thou preparest a table before me in the presence of mine enemies: thou anointest my head with oil; my cup runneth over. Surely goodness and mercy shall follow me all the days of my life: and I will dwell in the house of the Lord forever. Amen." Pastor Ferlon lowered his head, as we all did, for a few moments of solemn, silent prayer.

Slowly the citizens of E-Town took their leave, quietly returnin' to their lives. Clay, Brian,

Jeff, Carmen, and me stood next to Maria Cortez and her father Jose as they cried.

Maria caressed Samuel's casket and said, "He will never hurt you again, Samuelito. Go home to Heaven where I will see you again someday."

Brian, Carmen, and Jeff slowly walked away.

Clay put his hand on Maria's shoulder and said. "God bless you, Maria, Jose."

Maria spun around and hugged him tight, and I saw tears runnin' down Clay's cheeks. After a few moments they pulled apart and he forced a smile, wipin' away tears. "Go, have a good life now. One with peace." He turned around and walked down the hill.

"God bless you, Clay Allison." She looked at me and smiled. "And you. Truly you're the archangel Michael."

I shook my head and lowered my gaze. "No, Ma'am. I'm just a humble, mortal man. Nothin' more."

"Nonsense. You say that, but in my heart I know the truth. God has shown me." She took my hands in hers. "Where will you go now?"

I looked over at Tom's fresh grave. "I have to go break some terrible news to my friend's wife in El Paso. From there, I don't know. I reckon I'll be back to help Clay. Things are about to get real interestin' with the land grant."

She stretched up and kissed me on the cheek. "God bless you, Michael Angelico."

Chapter 13

Clay went on back to the ranch and continued workin'. I knew there was a war comin' too. He'd be ready, but I wouldn't be leavin' him shorthanded. After I went to do my duty in El Paso, I'd be back to help.

Maria eventually married a good man and had a life filled with peace and love. A life she deserved.

I never saw Brian again after all this, not sure what ever happened to him.

Davy came back and continued raisin' hell. I suppose we all did, to be honest.

I never saw Mister Mills again. I guess he decided he didn't want any more of us. None of us were ever charged with a crime.

Kennedy's head would stay on the post in front of Lambert's until it eventually mummified and disappeared. I suppose someone wanted a souvenir. The sign was gone in just a few days, probably for the same reason.

I had a mission to complete in El Paso. As the weather eased up I prepared for my journey south before the full winter hit. But not before returnin' to Carmen's place with a handful of dirty dishes.

We washed them together.

Grave Markers

Charles Kennedy's body was buried outside the E-Town city cemetery. His wooden grave marker read, 'CHARLES KENNEDY. BORN 1839, DIED Oct. 7 1870, Came to his death by hanging at the hands of parties unknown'.

Clay Allison died on July 3, 1887. His death was nothing to reflect the life he'd led. It was a simple accident. His grave stone read, 'ROBERT C ALLISON, CSA, CO F, 9th TENN CAV, SEP 2 1840, JUL 3 1887. GENTLEMAN GUN FIGHTER'. In addition, a second marker was placed at the foot of his grave which read, 'He never killed a man that did not need killing'.

Upon hearing of Clay's death, Maria Gregoria shed a tear, despite all the horrible things she'd heard about him since the events in E-Town. She knew he was not what they said. She knew he was much, much more. "Rest in peace, Clay Allison," she said.

Afterword
By Ron Washburn

There are quite a few similar accounts of the story of Charles Kennedy out there. A simple internet search of that name, or the names Clay Allison or Elizabethtown, New Mexico will yield a lot of reading material. What happened in October of 1870 in Elizabethtown, a story that was a precursor of sorts to the Colfax County War, has never been fully fleshed out. At least, not in my opinion nor satisfaction. So, I set myself to the task of finding out what really happened that cold autumn in northern New Mexico. Unfortunately, details were sketchy at best. Sometimes the internet doesn't know all, as I was led to believe.

But, after a few lengthy phone calls and a road trip to the area I wanted to write about, visiting the museum in Elizabethtown, I finally had a deeper understanding of the events.

It's taken me a while to work it all out, though. What was fiction and what was truth was the hardest to sift. There is the popular account of it that can be found with just the first layer of effort, but there was more that happened. Much, much more.

As a matter of fact, there was more than I was willing to write. Details that, although were correct for the most part, had little to do with the events I wanted to put down in a book. There are the back stories of all the main characters involved, for example. Who were Charles Kennedy, his wife, Clay Allison, Davy Crockett, and so on? Although this is interesting reading, it was for the most part irrelevant to this particular story.

All we really need are these facts: Charles Kennedy was a mountain man and, in a word, a psychopath. He was a murderer, a scammer and an opportunist. A user. In fact, Kennedy wasn't even his real name.

His wife was a woman named Maria Gregoria Cortez who had lost her mother when she was a child, to be raised by a father who could hardly take care of himself.

Clay Allison was a veteran of the Civil War who had his own issues, namely that of a volatile temper and a penchant for getting into big trouble. But, he also had a talent for getting out of it. He was a quick-draw gunslinger, the kind that old western legends are made of. Plenty has been written about him. Go look if you have a mind to. In this story I was only interested in his participation in the events portrayed.

Davy Crockett was the alleged nephew of the legendary frontiersman, who we all know. He also had a particular talent for getting into and out of trouble.

Oh, and one more. Mike Austin. Good luck finding anything on him. He's my own creation. He's a fictional character who I've picked to tell this tale in his own words. I toyed with doing it different ways, but ultimately chose this style for a bit more artistic freedom. Since he's my character, I know more about him than any of the others.

Armed with a voice and the facts of the story, I assembled them into a work of historical fiction. Why do it this way instead of a straight factual retelling of the events? Because that to me is boring. It's simply my own opinion. There's little to move the story along, and might as well be just an extended bullet list of events. A time line. If that's what you're looking for, look elsewhere. I chose to dramatize this story and put you right in the middle of it, riding along, watching through Mike's eyes as he dealt with a very real, but fictionalized, account.

What I'm trying to tell you is, yes. I was able to find some 'true accounts' of what happened. But, since nobody alive today was actually there to tell us first-hand what happened, and none of you reading this was there, who can say what exactly happened?

There are certainly some conflicting and confusing parts of this story, for example, how many children did Maria actually have, just to be killed by Charles? Was the same child who was killed in the first part of the book the same one who had been baptized roughly fifteen months earlier? (A matter of public record) I made a leap of fiction and placed 'Samuel' at three years old. But, if you follow the historical records, he was half that age. So, what's the truth? Were there possibly two children living there at the same time? One who died earlier (Samuel) and then an older one (Name unknown) who had his head bashed in? We may never know.

Who were Kennedy's victims? Do we have a list somewhere that we can refer to? Or does that even matter?

There are other parts of the official historical account that don't make sense, too, like Clay Allison taking Kennedy's head to Cimarron in a sack. Why would he do that? Was Kennedy actually beheaded? Was he drug to death or actually hanged? Neither? Both?

So, this was my goal: To tell you what we already know happened, and to tell you what probably happened, and to tell you what would have happened had it happened like it probably did.

ADDITIONAL READING

Books:

The Pain and the Sorrow, by Loretta Miles Tollefson, Sunstone Press, ISBN: 978-1632931849

Clay Allison: Legend of Cimmaron, by John A. Truett, Sunstone Press, ISBN: 978-0865343085

The Life and Death of a Gunfighter, Book 1, Part One: The Saga of Clay Allison/Gentlemen Gunfighter, by Gerry Allison, AuthorHouse, ISBN: 978-1403349552

Colfax County (Images of America), by Stephen Zimmer, Gene Lamm, Arcadia Publishing, ISBN: 1467133566

Web sites:

https://lorettamilestollefson.com/

https://www.legendsofamerica.com/we-charleskennedy/

https://www.amazon.com/author/ronwashburn

Made in the USA
Middletown, DE
28 August 2022

71504151R00113